Outstanding praise for the novels of Julia Templeton!

THE BARGAIN

"Very sensual and exciting. Renaud is male intensified, and Aleysia is just the woman to match him. If you like a sexy true-love story, I highly recommend this one."
—*Fresh Fiction*

"A passionate historical tale . . . breathtaking! When I see the name Julia Templeton on the cover of a historical novel, I know within the pages is an extraordinary read. *The Bargain* was that and more; it consumed me for hours! I had to know what was next for these wonderfully dynamic characters. I savored this book and know without a doubt I will read it time and again."
—*Romance Junkies*

"Julia Templeton will blow you away with her latest super-hot erotic historical *The Bargain*. The Norman conquest is the ideal backdrop for this tale of loyalty, love, and courage. Perfectly balanced with enough eroticism to keep your attention, strong dynamic characters, and a fascinating historical period. *The Bargain* is one of the best buys of the month."
—*A Romance Review*

"A heated historical . . . Fans of late eleventh-century romances with torrid love scenes will enjoy the star-crossed tale."
—*Midwest Book Review*

"Four stars! Templeton weaves a sensual spell over readers in this erotic romance set during the time of the Norman conquest of England. She does a fantastic job of slowly developing the love story between Aleysia and Renaud, making their affair and the steamy sex scenes even more exciting."
—*Romantic Times*

RETURN TO ME

"Templeton takes us on a journey of the heart . . . and she gives us a love story we will never forget! I am looking forward to taking Mrs. Templeton's next voyage, wherever that may lead."
—*Night Owl Romance*

"Templeton has taken a chance here—and it works. I was glad I encountered these characters, and I look forward to Templeton's next work in the hope that she will continue to defy the predictable and ordinary."
—*All About Romance*

"An exciting tale."
—*Midwest Book Review*

Books by Julia Templeton

SINJIN

VICTOR

Published by Kensington Publishing Corporation

VICTOR

JULIA TEMPLETON

APHRODISIA
KENSINGTON BOOKS
http://www.kensingtonbooks.com

APHRODISIA BOOKS are published by

Kensington Publishing Corp.
119 West 40th Street
New York, NY 10018

All Kensington Titles, Imprints, and Distributed Lines are available at special quantity discounts for bulk purchases for sales promotions, premiums, fund-raising, and educational or institutional use.

Special book excerpts or customized printings can also be created to fit specific needs. For details, write or phone the office of the Kensington special sales manager: Kensington Publishing Corp., 119 West 40th Street, New York, NY 10018, attn: Special Sales Department, Phone: 1-800-221-2647.

ISBN-13: 978-0-7582-3816-0
ISBN-10: 0-7582-3816-9

First Kensington Trade Paperback Printing: April 2010

10 9 8 7 6 5 4 3 2 1

Printed in the United States of America

To Toni and Patrice—
for always being there.

1

Victor Rayborne looked out over the grounds of his family's country estate. It had been a fortnight since his mother had made the announcement that he and his brothers must find brides or lose everything. His eldest sibling, Sinjin, had succeeded in winning the hand of the beautiful Katelyn Davenport, a woman who at the beginning of said party had been engaged to another man.

A man who now lay dead by his own hand.

Releasing a sigh, he scrubbed a hand over his face. Unlike his brother who had fallen in love so quickly, Victor had not found a woman who caught his fancy among the young debutantes that his mother had brought to Claymoore Hall. However, he had found a chaperone who intrigued him.

Lillith Winthrop, Lady Nordland, widow and aunt to Katelyn and her sister, Marilyn, was a beautiful blonde with striking hazel eyes and a body built for pleasure. The attraction had been instantaneous, and yet everything he'd heard about Lillith revolved around her virtuous reputation for being the very picture of decorum, an example of what every young lady should aspire to be.

In short, she was the opposite of what kind of woman he usually was attracted to. Actresses and dancers had always been his type, much like his last mistress, the beautiful twenty-five-year-old Selene.

The door to his chamber opened and his brother Rory appeared, his messy dark hair and rumpled appearance saying he'd just come from a liaison. Rory had been gifted with striking good looks that women found irresistible. When he entered a room, men held tight to their wives, daughters, and mistresses.

"You look like hell. Where have you been?"

Rory flashed a wolfish smile. "With the incomparable Lady Anna."

Lady Anna had entertained both Victor and Rory in her chamber just days into the party. Since that event he had steered clear of the woman, but apparently Rory could not get enough of the sexually voracious young lady. "I'm surprised her chaperone has not caught on yet."

"Yes, well, there is something to be said about having a chaperone who is hard of hearing and has weak eyesight." Rory fell into a chair beside the fireplace.

"Perhaps you should ask Lady Anna to marry you?"

Rory snorted. "Anna is an excellent lover, to be sure, but I cannot imagine her as a wife. I could never trust her."

"Isn't that a bit like the pot calling the kettle black?"

"Yes, well . . ." Rory brushed his hands through his hair and yawned loudly. "What of you? I noticed you dancing with a certain widow last night. Do I sense interest on your part?"

His brothers knew him better than anyone, so it was no use denying it. "Yes, I find Lillith intriguing."

"She's lovely. Hard to believe she's the aunt. I would have

taken her more as the sister, especially given that remarkable figure," Rory said, a smile on his face. "Oh, and you'll love this; Lady Anna says that Lillith is unattainable."

Unattainable? Ironically, the news fascinated him even more. A woman as beautiful as Lillith, and a wealthy, titled widow at that, should have men beating down her door. Chances were she wasn't interested. Little wonder given what he now knew of her husband.

Every time he approached Lillith she looked ready to bolt—until last night. Last night he had sensed a change in her when they danced. She had laughed and smiled the entire time. He did take into account that said happiness could have been more about the fact that her niece had become engaged and less about her dancing partner, but he'd felt elated nonetheless.

"Oh my God, you really like her." Rory sat up straight now. "I'll wager you one hundred pounds that you can't get her into bed."

A part of Victor rebelled at making such a wager, yet the rake in him couldn't resist the challenge. He and Rory had always had a strange rivalry, and it's not like this would be the first time they'd bet on getting a woman into bed. "Make it your gold pocket watch and we have a deal."

Rory frowned. "The one Grandfather gave me?"

"Yes, the very one, which you never wear." Victor had secretly coveted the piece for years. When Rory had received the treasured antique after their grandfather's passing, he had been crushed. He shouldn't have been so surprised since Rory had always been their grandfather's golden boy.

Rory's eyes narrowed as he contemplated the wager, and Victor had a sneaking suspicion he would not go for it, when finally Rory released an exasperated sigh, stood, and extended his hand. "Very well, you shall have the pocket watch, but only if you seduce Lady Nordland. And you will not just bed her and be done with it, but rather captivate her completely and make her your mistress."

Victor wasn't sure about his ability to "captivate her completely" and make her his mistress, but bedding her he could do, despite the fact her flawless reputation suggested otherwise.

He shook Rory's hand. "Done," he said with more confidence than he felt.

Lillith lifted her face to the sun. It was a glorious day, and she felt extremely gratified as she watched her niece Katelyn and her fiancé Sinjin walk hand in hand along the grounds under the watchful eye of Sinjin's proud mother, Lady Rochester.

Any misgivings the countess might have had about her eldest son marrying Katelyn had apparently been put aside, for she positively beamed as she took tea with her friends.

If only Marilyn had found love with one of the Rayborne brothers or one of their male guests, then the party would have been an even greater success. For a short while Lillith thought her niece had fallen in love with Victor, especially when she had happened upon them kissing in the labyrinth.

However, Marilyn had assured her that Victor was nothing more than a friend. Lillith didn't push for more answers, as a part of her honestly didn't want to know the truth. Admittedly, she'd been more than a little jealous when she'd witnessed the kiss, and worried that both she and her niece had feelings for the renowned rakehell.

Victor was a decade younger than Lillith, in his prime, and he made her feel small and feminine, and yes, even desired—something she had not felt for many, many years. True, she had been pursued by older gentlemen intent on taking a well-respected widow as their wife, but none of those men thrilled her the way Victor Rayborne did.

Victor brought out something in her that made her feel like

a girl again. Indeed, he made her wonder what it would be like to behave badly; a new concept given she had spent the past two decades playing the elegant, loyal, ever virtuous wife to a detestable man who paraded his many male lovers before her.

She had hoped to have children of her own, but her fifteen-year marriage had yielded no such blessing. Little wonder given her husband had rarely visited her bed. The night of her wedding had been the stuff of nightmares, and she had come to hate Winfred's drunken visits. What a fantastic actor he had been during their courtship. If she could have only guessed that behind the sheep's clothing lay a malicious wolf, she would have run for her life.

But there was no use in crying over what had happened. Those days were long behind her. She could only move on to what could be.

"Lady Nordland," a deep voice said from behind her, and she turned slowly.

Victor's brilliant blue eyes slid down her body and up again. His dark, wavy hair fell to his broad shoulders in wild disarray, and he had the most arresting features: square jaw, jutting cheekbones, and lovely full lips. He was dressed in black from his shirt and snug trousers that hugged muscular thighs to the slightly worn Hessians. The dark attire made his light eyes even more vivid, she realized.

"Lord Graston, good afternoon." She managed to keep her tone casual; a difficult feat when exhilaration rushed through her veins, making her heart pound as if she'd run a race.

"May I?" he asked, motioning to the chair beside her.

She nodded, "Of course."

He sat in the chair, his long legs stretching out before him. He made her thoughts turn positively scandalous, and she wondered if the rumors she had heard this past week were true: Lord Graston was a gracious, extremely well-endowed lover with incredible stamina and skill. A flash of what he must look like naked came to mind and Lillith shifted in her seat. Truth be told, she had never been so attracted to a man in all her thirty-eight years.

Nearby, someone laughed aloud and Lillith straightened her spine. She glanced at a nearby table to see a young woman and her chaperone watching her closely and talking behind their fans. The chaperone lifted a brow as though to say, "Who do you think you are, you old maid?" Indeed, were they laughing at her because Victor was showing interest, or that she was so obviously taken with him?

"Lily, Lily, Lily, when will you stop worrying about what others are thinking or saying?" Victor whispered, his voice far too intimate.

"I am a chaperone, Lord Graston. And people talk if said chaperone, and a widow at that, spends too much time in the company of a single, young man."

He sighed heavily. "Who cares what they say? Let them speculate."

If only it were that easy. She didn't want to destroy her hard-earned reputation in a few days' time. And yet, he was right. Why was it that she always worried about what others thought of her? Perhaps in the past it had been because she'd tried to save herself the humiliation of a horrific marriage and a husband who despised her. She had wanted to be liked so desperately that she had lived her life as an example of what a woman should be.

And she was bloody miserable.

"You are leaving today?" he asked, his voice hinting at disappointment.

"We had planned to, but my nieces have talked me into staying on another day."

His face lit up and her pulse skittered. "I am glad to hear it.

Perhaps your nieces will persuade you into staying another week."

Honestly, she would not mind staying another week, but she feared spending seven more days in this man's company. It was not so much that she did not trust him, but rather, she did not trust herself. "I am afraid a week is out of the question," she said, feeling a blush work its way up her neck. "I have obligations I must attend to in London."

"Can I visit you in London?" he asked so nonchalantly he might have been talking about the weather.

It was not unusual for her to welcome friends and new acquaintances to her home, but usually those "friends" were women, not men. Her neighbors would be all aflutter if a handsome young man started calling on her.

"We will be family soon, Lily," he said, as though reading her thoughts. "You need not worry what others would think."

Yes, they would be family soon; but given his reputation, no one would misconstrue what his visits meant. "Of course you can visit me in London, but I thought you were returning to Rochester."

"I am, indeed, returning to Rochester, but not for long." His gaze shifted from her lips to her breasts. "I suddenly have a strong desire to see London again."

Her stomach tightened as his gaze shifted back to hers. She understood innuendos well enough—the heated glint in his gaze, the way his stare burned into her, down her body, taking everything in with a glance. The question was why, when he had a bevy of beautiful young women at his disposal, all aching for the chance to get to know him better in the hopes of marrying him, did he want to spend time with her, an old widow. *A barren widow,* she thought with growing dismay.

"Will you not ask me why I have such a strong desire to see London again?"

He could be so very exasperating! "Very well, Lord Graston, *why* do you yearn to see London again so soon after leaving?"

He reached for her hand, his long fingers sliding between hers. "Because I want to be near you, Lily. I would follow you to the ends of the earth if need be."

She knew the ways of rakes and scoundrels well enough—all the charming phrases they used in order to get what they wanted. *Do women actually fall for this drivel?* she wondered.

His piercing, long-lashed eyes held her pinned to the spot and she found it very difficult to breathe. Apparently, she was not so very different from other women who had fallen victim to his charm.

She abruptly pulled her hand away, hoping that no one else had seen the exchange.

Victor's lips quirked. "You have grown quiet, Lily."

"Have I?" she asked, her voice coming out harsher than intended. "I suppose I do not know what you want me to say. A part of me wonders if you are toying with me."

"Why would I toy with you, Lily?"

It seemed that he enjoyed making her uncomfortable. The main objective was to not let him affect her, or at the very least not let him know he affected her. "It goes without saying that your parents want you to marry, and I am obviously not the best choice."

His brows rose. "Why would that be?"

She cleared her throat. "I am widowed, and I am—a good deal older than you."

"I have had many lovers older than yourself," he said, his eyes intense as he stared at her.

The admission made her strangely intrigued and set her mind at ease. She had not planned on getting into such an intimate discussion with him, but it was comforting to know that he'd had lovers older than she.

Feeling warmer by the second, Lillith reached for her fan. Flicking it open, she waved it vigorously in order to cool her heated cheeks. Good Lord, she was beginning to perspire, and the more he stared, the more uncomfortable she became.

He leaned near and whispered in her ear, "Perhaps I can visit your bedchamber this evening?"

The breath lodged in her throat. Clearly she had not heard him correctly? Who would be so bold as to ask to visit her bedchamber? A rakehell, that's who. "I do believe you are trying to unnerve me, Lord Graston."

His grin was altogether devastating, his eyes heavy lidded and suggestive, and for a breathless moment she envisioned him naked, making love to her with expert skill, bringing her to climax for the first time with his well-endowed manhood. Heat swept through her body, making her nipples pebble against her bodice and the flesh between her thighs tingle.

It seemed he could read her every wicked thought, because as he watched her watch him, his smile deepened. Oh, but he was all confidence and pomp. "And am I succeeding in unnerving you, Lily?"

He rested his elbow on the arm of the chair and brushed his thumb over his full lower lip. The movement was strangely sensual, which did not help her current state of arousal in the least.

She sat up straighter and squared her shoulders. "Lord Graston, certainly there is another woman present who might be more receptive to your invitation."

"I think you are receptive, Lily. I think you want to be made love to and let your inhibitions go. Have you not wondered what it would be like to have a lover warm your bed? A younger lover who would appreciate you and perhaps even surprise you in the bedchamber."

The blood in her veins positively burned. She waved her fan faster and tried without success to dislodge the wicked images racing through her mind.

His gaze wandered over her face, down to the low neckline of her gown. "I wonder what you would look like with your hair down, the curls spilling over my pillow in wild disarray, and your luscious naked body wrapped in my sheets."

The passionate look in his eyes and the sensual tone of his voice were too much. Though no one sat close enough to hear their discussion, she was aware that they were being watched. Feeling trapped, she stood so fast she nearly upended the chair in her haste. She stopped herself before she stormed off. A lady never made a scene. She forced a smile and gave a curt nod. "Lord Graston, it was a pleasure."

"I have upset you." It wasn't a question, and to her surprise, the devilish smile had disappeared.

"I am unaccustomed to being talked to in such a manner, Lord Graston. I am no whore."

Oh dear. Victor had hit a nerve.

"Forgive me, Lady Nordland. I only know what others have said, and I understand your husband was not—the most gracious of husbands." Victor regretted the words the moment they left his mouth, and even more so when Lillith's mouth formed an O. Seconds later, she snapped her mouth shut, turned on her heel, and left him staring after her.

He pondered his choices: he could let her cool off and try and talk to her later, or he could settle matters now. Aware they had an audience, his mother included, he stood slowly and walked in the opposite direction Lillith had gone as not to cause further speculation.

Avoiding eye contact at all costs, he continued at a leisurely pace until he rounded the manor, at which time he raced to the servants' entrance. The stairwell was narrow and steep. Taking the steps two at a time, he made it to the second floor and smiled to himself upon seeing Lillith just stepping onto the landing. Her chin was lifted high, shoulders straight and rigid, her steps rushed.

She was clearly furious.

He caught up with her instantly and was within arm's reach when he said her name.

She stopped abruptly, so fast he nearly ran into her back.

She took a deep breath and turned.

His stomach tightened. Her expression was as cold as ice.

"I wanted to apologize to you," he blurted, shocked to see disdain in her eyes. Where had the amiable widow gone? "I did not mean to come across so—"

"Arrogant? Callous? Rude?" she said through clenched teeth.

Oh my. The lady had a bit of fire in her, after all. He opened his mouth to defend himself, then closed it just as quickly.

Her beautiful hazel eyes widened as she waited for his explanation.

"Yes, I am all of those things and more," he said, choosing his words carefully. "I meant no disrespect, Lady Nordland. I feel comfortable with you. Perhaps more comfortable than I should be, and I oftentimes speak my mind without thought of consequence. I am sincerely sorry if I offended you in any way. I can assure you that it will not happen again."

Her cheeks were flushed, her eyes sparkling with anger. He wanted desperately to throw her over his shoulder, take her to his room, and make love to her until she couldn't stand.

"Well, I accept your apology," she said, her tongue sliding over her bottom lip.

Oh, she shouldn't have done that. He ached to taste those

soft rose pink lips, to nibble at them, and do innumerable things to that mouth. He could already anticipate sliding his cock past—

"Is that all, Lord Graston?" she asked, a tawny brow lifting as she awaited his response.

"No," he said. Unable to resist any longer, he took a step closer and pulled her against him.

Her fan fell to the ground and she gasped, looking up at him with a mixture of shock and a cross between horror and excitement.

"I've wanted to kiss you from the moment I met you," he whispered against her lips, before kissing her softly.

Their breath mingled, and he could feel her heart racing against his own. Tentatively, he kissed her again, gently. When she didn't pull away, he slowly deepened the kiss, his tongue teasing the seam of her lips.

To his surprise, her hands slid to his chest, where she fisted the material of his shirt. Her mouth opened wider, her tongue sweeping against his as she leaned against him fully.

Sweet acceptance.

She moaned—the sound like music to his ears.

He held her tight to him: one hand at the small of her back, the other weaving through the curls at the nape of her neck. As the kiss became more heated, his hand moved lower, over her soft, rounded, and incredibly firm buttocks.

Apparently he was moving too fast because she wrenched away from him, her eyes wide with alarm as she stared at him like he'd suddenly sprouted wings.

A slender hand covered her mouth and she blinked in disbelief.

"Lily," he said, reaching out for her, wanting to rekindle the fire, but she shook her head.

"I'm sorry, I can't do this," she said, taking a step away from him. Then she turned and ran.

2

Lillith wanted to leave Claymoore Hall immediately.

Unfortunately, her nieces did not feel the same, and when she told them she wanted to leave first thing in the morning, both protested heartily.

But she would stand firm in her decision. They were leaving tomorrow, and nothing would change her mind. To stay at Claymoore Hall was foolhardy, and honestly she did not know if she had the willpower to stay away from Victor Rayborne.

When he had kissed her, her bones had felt like they were melting, and a thousand emotions had riddled her, most of all desire. Victor's very presence was like an aphrodisiac to her senses. He was temptation incarnate, and she had never wanted anyone so badly.

But the last thing she needed to do was make an ass out of herself in front of others she respected. And what would her nieces think of her gallivanting with Victor right beneath their noses when she was here to chaperone them, and when he clearly should be courting someone his own age or younger?

Yes, she needed to leave tomorrow, and she could not let Katelyn or Marilyn convince her otherwise.

She had considered staying in her chamber for the duration of the evening, but she had never been one to hide. She had faced her husband each night at dinner, as well as his lovers on many occasions. So why could she not face a young man who had kissed her senseless hours earlier? A man who made her thoughts turn positively scandalous.

Instead of cowering away like a wallflower, she would venture downstairs, join the others, and act as though the earlier event in the hallway had not transpired.

And she had dressed accordingly, wearing the most modest gown she had brought with her. The dress had a conservative neckline, long sleeves, and was a yellowish green that did not exactly do her coloring justice. Her sister, Loraine, had once told her this particular shade "washed her out." She gripped the door handle when she thought of the beautiful sapphire silk gown with lovely embroidered detail at the low neckline she had brought along but had not worn.

No, she would not give in and change. She was making a point, if not to Victor, then to herself. Plus, she did not want to come across like she was actually trying to gain his attention.

As she approached the parlor, she very nearly talked herself out of attending dinner. Perhaps she should rush back up the stairs to the sanctuary of her bedchamber and let them all think she had a headache. Perhaps no one would notice, save for her nieces.

The door to the parlor opened, and upon seeing her, a servant held the door open and motioned her in.

Damn.

Taking a steadying breath, Lillith entered the room.

She saw Katelyn immediately, standing beside Sinjin, who was speaking to an older gentleman.

Her eldest niece looked youthful in a pastel gown that complemented her auburn hair and green eyes. Her porcelain skin was the envy of many a woman of the *ton,* and Lillith smiled with pride.

Katelyn grinned as she approached. "Aunt Lily, I am so glad you came down," she said, kissing each cheek. "I was just telling Marilyn that we needed to check on you."

"I am sorry I worried you both. Time got away from me," she said, feeling bad for the small lie. "Where is your sister?"

"She went to get a shawl. She said she was cool."

"I hope she is not ill."

"Not at all, Aunt. You know Marilyn. She is always cold when the rest of us are too warm. She will be down momentarily." Katelyn shifted on her feet, and Lillith knew her niece had something on her mind.

Sinjin shook the hand of the man he'd been talking with and turned to Lillith. "Lady Nordland, might I be the first to say how lovely you look this evening."

The Rayborne brothers were all gorgeous to a fault. Each tall, dark, and strikingly handsome. "Thank you, my lord."

"I will give you two a moment alone," he said, kissing Katelyn.

"Why do I feel like you have something to ask me?" Lillith asked, knowing what was to come. She had to stay strong and not let herself be talked into doing what she did not want to do.

"Sinjin wants me to remain at Claymoore Hall for a few more days. I was hoping you would agree to stay with me."

Lillith straightened her shoulders. She needed to get away from Claymoore Hall fast, and no amount of begging or pleading from her nieces would change that. "I do need to return to London, my dear. I wish we could stay, but I do not see where that is possible."

Katelyn looked devastated. Her niece had been through so

much with the recent demise of her fiancé, Lord Balliford, a detestable man hand-picked by her mother, who had taken his own life just days ago.

"And given Lord Balliford's recent death, I think it is in your best interest to return with me to London." Lillith cleared her throat. "Staying is not an option."

"Just one more day, Aunt Lily. Please . . ."

How desperate she sounded.

"I understand your disappointment, my darling," Lillith said, avoiding her niece's pout. "But before you know it, you will be married and spending every day of your life with Sinjin."

Katelyn nodded, though the words did not ease her discouragement. "I know that Marilyn wishes to stay as well."

Bloody hell.

Her tone was hopeful, as was her expression.

"Let me think on it, my dear," Lillith replied, trying without success to hide her irritation.

"Thank you, Aunt Lily. You have been so wonderful and understanding this past week. I will always be forever grateful for your presence here."

"Flattery will get you nowhere, Kate," Lillith said, scanning the crowd. She was grateful to see the size of the party had shrunk considerably. Only thirty or so guests remained, many of whom sat talking amongst themselves. A violinist played at the far end of the room, and Lillith's heart gave a jolt when she recognized Victor's broad shoulders. He sat on a settee with his back to her, beside the beautiful Lady Anna. The two seemed completely enamored of each other, their laughter loud and boisterous.

Lillith did not know what to make of the young woman who had befriended her nieces. Anna was outspoken, charismatic, and could flirt as well as any man twice her age, but the stories she had heard this past week were a bit disconcerting.

And it didn't help that the young woman's disappearance from events had been noted, that along with certain young gentlemen.

Victor slid an arm on the back of the settee, his fingers nearly brushing the other woman's neck. Much like he had touched Lillith's neck earlier when he had kissed her.

Foolish woman, she thought to herself, looking away from the cozy duo. Victor had wanted to add Lillith to his long list of conquests and nothing more. No doubt he would be elated to see her leave Claymoore Hall, despite their earlier conversation where he'd asked her to stay.

"Aunt Lily," Katelyn said, and Lillith glanced at her niece, who watched her with a quizzical expression. "I asked if you wished to take a walk in the gardens later with me and Sinjin. There is to be a full moon this evening."

"How lovely. Yes, of course, I would be delighted to join you. When your sister returns, be sure to ask Marilyn to accompany us."

"She's already agreed."

"Excellent."

Rory stepped into the room, fixing the lace at his cuffs. The youngest Rayborne brother was so incredibly good looking that one could not help but stare. He stood as tall as Victor, and just as broad at the shoulders, but was perhaps a bit more muscular than either of his brothers. A natural athlete, and infamous flirt, he made women all around him giggle like schoolgirls. Every single woman in the room, including Anna, looked at Rory.

When he walked toward Lillith, she straightened. They had had only a few conversations, and those had been limited in length.

"Good evening, ladies," Rory said, lifting Katelyn's hand in his own and bringing it to his lips, before greeting Lillith in the same manner. "How are you, Lady Nordland?"

His gaze met hers, and her heart actually missed a beat. He had lovely blue eyes, and his smile could only be described as wolfish. "Very well, thank you," she replied.

"I am so glad your nieces talked you into staying another night at Claymoore Hall. I do so hope you will consider staying longer."

"Mr. Rayborne, I do believe my nieces are conspiring against me, for Katelyn has just asked me that very question."

"We are hoping to talk her into at least one more night," Katelyn said, looking at Lillith with that damnable hopeful expression.

"Then you really must stay, Lily."

He practically purred her name.

"Well, we shall see."

"My brother will be very pleased to hear you are considering staying."

She wondered which brother he referred to but decided against asking. Instead, she smiled tightly and glanced over at Victor, who was pulling himself away from Anna.

Then he was walking toward Lillith, and his gaze shifted over her in a slow, and what she guessed to be, deliberate way that had her pulse racing. The side of his lips quirked, and she was reminded of her modest choice of gown. Did that sly smile mean he knew she had dressed plainly on purpose?

Instead of hiding behind a conservative gown, she should have thrown caution to the wind and worn something gorgeous and attractive . . . like the sapphire dress hanging in the wardrobe. She wondered if he was thanking his lucky stars she had denied him.

Rory glanced at his brother and the two shared a conspiratorial smile, and was that a wink? Lillith's stomach clenched, wondering if Victor had told Rory about the kiss.

Marilyn rushed up from behind him and Lillith was grateful for her arrival.

"Good evening, ladies," he said, greeting Katelyn and Marilyn with kisses to their hands. When he came to Lillith, he lifted her hand, his fingers sliding over her palm as he brought it slowly to his lips.

Lillith saw the mirrored smiles on her nieces' faces and nearly ripped her hand free of Victor's. However, doing so would only make her appear childish and imprudent, and that would not do.

"Lady Nordland, may I escort you to dinner?" he asked, already extending his elbow for her to take.

"Of course," she murmured, ignoring the gleeful expressions on Katelyn's and Marilyn's faces.

Lillith's heart roared in her ears as they passed by a chaperone not much older than she. Lillith could plainly see the condemnation—or perhaps it was jealousy in the other woman's eyes. Would she feel likewise if the tables were turned?

They walked out into the hallway and into the dining room. The long, opulent table was beautiful with a cream-colored lace tablecloth, fashionable china arranged precisely, and ornate candelabras spaced every few feet apart. A fire blazed in the fireplace, and already conversation filled the room.

"Sit here," Victor said, sliding a chair out for her.

"Is there a seating arrangement?"

"Yes, and luckily my mother had the foresight to seat you beside me." He flashed a smile, and for the first time she realized he had dimples.

"Yes, well . . . I wonder," Lillith said. Her tone must have lacked civility because a moment later he looked her in the eye, his expression impassive.

"Do you wish to sit somewhere else, Lady Nordland?" he asked, sounding and looking injured.

Feeling bad, she shook her head. "Of course not, Lord Graston. I always enjoy your company." Especially when he pulled her into his arms and kissed her senseless.

His brilliant blue eyes held hers intently. Good Lord, his lashes were obscenely long and thick. Long and thick . . . much like a part of his anatomy was rumored to be.

Uncomfortable with the bold stare and the scandalous direction of her thoughts, she folded her hands in her lap as Victor sat beside her, pulling his chair in.

Both her nieces sat near the far end of the table, close to Lady Rochester, Sinjin, and Lady Anna, whom Marilyn was conversing with. The two young women had grown quite close over the past week, and Lillith worried about the acquaintance given the other woman's sordid reputation.

"Wine?" a servant asked, and Lillith shook her head.

"Come, Lily, live a little." Victor's sarcastic tone held a challenge.

"On second thought, I shall," she said to the servant, who filled the glass nearly to the rim.

Beside her, Victor grinned and lifted his glass. "To your health."

She lifted her glass and clicked it against his. "To your health."

He stared at her with that boyish smile that made her shift in her seat. Did he not realize how uncomfortable that stare made her?

She brought the glass to her lips and took a small sip. Long fingers brushed against her thigh, to the curve of her leg and hip.

Setting the glass down before she toppled it, she nodded at the woman across the table from her and proceeded to push Victor's hand away with her right hand. For all the good it did. His hand returned immediately to her thigh.

God help her, but it was going to be a long night.

He leaned close and whispered in her ear, "That gown reveals how large your breasts are. Impressive for such a small frame."

Her nipples pebbled against the fabric, sensitive and aching. To her horror, an image of Victor standing before her naked as the day he'd been born flashed before her, and her cheeks turned hot. How could she possibly get through this night? she wondered, shifting in her seat. Perhaps she should excuse herself and plead a headache.

Rory came up from behind them, nearly scaring Lillith out of her skin. She felt her cheeks grow warmer by the second and reached for the wine. Anything to keep herself occupied. Rory's gaze skipped to her lap for only an instant. He had to see his brother's hand there. Her thoughts were confirmed when seconds later he smiled. "How are you doing this evening, Lady Nordland?" he asked, his hands on the back of her chair.

"Very well, thank you."

"Is my brother bothering you?"

"Only a little," she said teasingly, and wondered what in the hell she was thinking by saying as much.

Truth be told, she found both Victor and Rory arrogant and altogether too confident. A bit too much like her husband . . .

"So have you decided if you will be staying on with us, Lady Nordland?" Rory asked, and Lillith shook her head.

"No, I must return to London in the morning."

"So sorry to hear that," Rory replied, patting Victor on the shoulder, which again made Lillith wonder what the two were about. "Perhaps you'll have a change of heart.

"Perhaps." Lillith was grateful when Lady Rochester hit her spoon against her glass, signaling for the servants to begin the first course.

Thankfully, the gentleman to Lillith's left kept her conversing between courses. However, the redhead sitting to Victor's right, now dominated his time and conversation. As the woman's tone began to take on a soft, sultry quality, Lillith actually started to feel jealous.

As though sensing her annoyance, Victor's hand slipped to Lillith's leg.

Her muscles tensed as he moved ever closer to the juncture between her thighs.

Certainly he would not dare . . .

She checked the napkin, making sure it had not slipped from her lap.

His hand slid beneath the napkin.

She dared a sidelong glance at him. He still conversed with the redhead beside him, but he was slouched farther down in the chair, allowing him easier access to her lap.

Her thighs clamped tightly together.

Her efforts did not deter him. In fact, his questing fingers continued their path downward, his middle finger finding the tight bundle of nerves at the top of her sex. He grazed her tiny button, circling it with his fingertip, and her breath left her in a rush.

He was relentless, asserting more pressure, making her hotter and wetter by the second. She wanted to push his hand away, yet couldn't bring herself to do so.

Feeling her cheeks grow warmer by the second, she dared a glance at those around her, and thankfully, everyone appeared to be occupied in conversation.

She pushed at his hand and to her relief, Victor's hand fell away from her and he lifted his goblet with his other hand, took a long drink, and then set it down. Fingers that had been touching her slid along his lower lip, beneath his nose.

Scandalous man.

The redhead went back to eating and he leaned toward Lillith. "How is the duck?" he asked, his blue eyes sparkling with devious intent.

She hadn't even touched her plate, but his question sent her into motion. "Very well, thank you." Her voice sounded husky and shaky, even to her own ears.

A servant chose that moment to set dessert before her.

She drank her entire glass of wine and even motioned for the footman to fill it again, the libation effectively easing the tension boiling within her.

Tomorrow she would leave Claymoore Hall and this would all be nothing but a memory.

Down the table she caught Katelyn's gaze. Her niece smiled and Lillith's heart gave a jolt before she looked up at Sinjin. Her niece wanted to stay with her intended, that much was obvious. Oh to be so young and in love. Lillith remembered how she had felt when Winfred had started courting her. The pulse-pounding excitement, the anticipation of what it would be like to be made love to . . . and what it had felt like to have the rug ripped out from underneath her.

Lillith folded her hands in her lap, melancholy washing over her when Victor reached for her, his fingers curling around hers. He squeezed her hand and her throat tightened.

She savored the feeling of skin against skin. Everything about him consumed her. Indeed, she could smell his cologne; the sandalwood mixed with the heady scent that was all his own.

He made her feel so unlike herself—and she didn't know if that was good or bad.

3

Victor could see and feel Lillith's agitation as his hand slid back to her lap, his fingers squeezing her thigh.

True, he had been rather obtuse in touching her beneath the table, but she had borne it with the dignity of the lady that she was. Even now, she did not pull away from his touch, though her hands remained firmly clasped in her lap, her chin lifted high, her shoulders rigid.

Ever the lady.

She took a deep breath, the action making her chest rise and fall heavily. He knew she had gone out of her way to dress the part of the respectable widow, but if she thought to thwart his desire by covering her incredible body in fashions befitting someone more than twenty years her age, then she was sadly mistaken.

The game was on.

The redhead to his right had started to play a game of her own, her stockinged foot caressing his foot, sliding up toward his ankle, to curl around his calf.

At any other time he would be amused and even intrigued

by the young lady's boldness, but given how badly he wanted the lady to his left, he wanted none of it. He ever so gently moved his foot a good inch or so to the left.

He caught her sidelong glance, the creasing between her brows as she frowned at him, obviously not understanding why he was not reciprocating. Apparently, she was determined, because she tried coaxing him again. He sat back in his chair, took a deep breath, and glanced at her.

She flashed him a coquettish smile.

He might have to be blunt, he thought to himself as her foot returned to his, her toes inching up his shin. A second later, her hand moved from the table to his thigh.

His throat went dry. Had the little vixen seen him touch Lillith? Is that why all the sudden she was doing the same to him?

Her hand moved up his thigh, grazing his cock, which remained surprisingly unaffected by her questing fingers. Now had it been Lillith touching him, perhaps there would have been a different response.

"Lord Graston, I wonder if you would be interested in a walk about the gardens after dinner," the redhead said, her lips curving into a smile that promised innumerable carnal delights if he were to join her.

He heard Lillith sigh heavily beside him and he glanced her way. Her cheeks were flushed, her jaw clenched tight. Was she jealous, he wondered, intrigued by the notion that she might be.

Perhaps he was getting through to her, after all.

"It is a bit blustery outside, my dear. Perhaps another time?"

The redhead looked astounded he would deny her.

"Or we could take a turn about the parlor later?" he said in the hopes to appease her.

Her hand did not move from his cock as he had hoped. Rather, she tried harder, her fingers tightening around his shaft.

To his surprise, Lillith's hand curled around his own, but he realized too late her intent. She ever so slightly moved his hand away, back to his lap, and to his dismay, her fingers brushed right against the redhead's adventurous hand.

Lillith ripped her hand away as though she'd been burned, and the redhead snatched hers away as well. Victor could only hope the vixen did not share any details with her friends, or Lady Nordland's reputation would be severely compromised.

Victor looked at the redhead and her brows were lifted high in surprise.

Oh dear.

This was not good, and there was not a lot, if anything, he could say in order to make it right.

Lillith sat at the vanity, brushing out her hair. It was not quite midnight, and already she had her bags packed and sitting beside the door, ready for her departure in the morning.

She was positively horrified at what she had allowed to happen during dinner. As if her own lack of judgment hadn't been bad enough, feeling the redhead's hand on Victor's crotch had been utterly degrading.

No wonder his wicked ways were so renowned. And to think for a few moments she had allowed herself to believe he actually might feel something for her.

Had Victor been touching the other woman beneath the table too? Perhaps he had been so determined not to go to bed alone that he had literally tried his hand at pawing both of them beneath the table, and it had been the redhead who had reciprocated.

Unfortunately for Lillith, the other woman had felt her hand when she had shoved Victor's hand back at him, and if she didn't keep her mouth closed about the whole ordeal, then everyone would be whispering about her come morning.

Which was why she must leave.

But if she left in the morning, would the redhead think she had fled because of the incident? If she stayed, then at least she could stand up for herself, and perhaps explain the situation.

She ran a trembling hand down her face. Perhaps she *should* stay? Lord knows her nieces would both be relieved.

Bloody hell, she was so confused! Why oh why had she gone down to dinner? She should have known Victor would try something scandalous.

She hated to admit it to herself, but when she had left the dining room directly after the final course was served, she had half expected Victor to follow her. But aside from saying her name in exasperation, he had stayed put. No doubt his other companion had jumped at the chance to be with him and join him for the night.

A knock sounded at the door and Lillith set the brush on the vanity's marble surface.

Certain it was one of her nieces come to check in with her, she crossed the room, not bothering to stop long enough to put on her robe.

She opened the door, the welcoming smile dying on her lips when she saw Victor standing before her. His blue eyes slid slowly over her body and back up again. She crossed her arms over her chest.

The cut of the chemise was modest enough, so she knew he could not see much, though the curving of his lips made her wonder if perhaps he could see through the material.

"May I come in?" he asked, making eye contact once again.

She did not want any of the other guests to see him standing in her doorway at this hour, nor did she want anyone to see him walking into her bedchamber.

His lips quirked and she wondered if he had the ability to

read minds. She took a step back and motioned for him to enter. Sliding on her robe, she belted it and turned to face him.

"I knew your hair would be beautiful down, flowing about your shoulders. The shade is lovely, and the texture like silk." He reached for a lock, then curled it around a finger. "I want to bury my face in the curls."

She swallowed hard and walked away from him, trying to dislodge the mental image his words caused. "So . . . what is it you want, Lord Graston?"

"I've already told you what I want, Lillith."

Her pulse skittered as he approached her, and she knew what prey must feel like being stalked by a predator.

She tried to collect her scattered wits, but it was so difficult. He was so tempting. Perhaps it was the wine that had made her so complacent. "I thought you would be with your dinner companion."

"I want you, Lily."

His words made her stomach tighten. "I felt her hand on you."

"I did not encourage her to touch me."

"I find that hard to believe given that you were groping me beneath the table," Lillith said, unable to keep the venom from her voice. She brushed trembling hands over her face. He unnerved her to no end.

"Tell me to leave, Lily, and I shall. I'll never bother you again."

She opened her mouth, ready to tell him to leave, but closed it just as quickly. Did she want him to never bother her again? Truth be told, his interest in her had been exhilarating. In fact, she'd felt young again, desirable, something she had not felt in more years than she could recall.

Reaching out, he slid his hand across her jaw, his large hand cupping her cheek, long fingers sliding into her hair, bracing her head as he leaned in for a kiss.

He consumed her, his intoxicating scent making her pulse leap with excitement. She wanted him. She wanted this, and she had fought her attraction for him from the very beginning.

His lips were soft, yet firm, tasting, teasing, before his tongue slid along the seam, seeking entry.

He held her tightly and walked until her back made contact with the bed, then followed her down onto the mattress.

She sighed and fought a thousand different emotions. The proper, virtuous lady inside her said to run while she could, yet the woman inside her couldn't move if she tried. There was no place she would rather be.

Every inch of his hard muscled body pressed against her. Lillith savored the sensations as she arched her hips against his huge cock. Heat rushed through her body, centering at the flesh between her legs. She was so wet, so sensitive, and as he cupped his hips, she moaned into his mouth.

Victor was shocked at the passionate woman beneath him. The way Lillith returned his kisses with such fervor, the way her nails dug into his shoulders, and the way she arched against him, her hips moving in a suggestive way, were things he'd expect from a mistress.

Reaching down between them, he lifted the chemise, his hands brushing along the silky-soft skin of her calf, her knee, and inner thighs.

Her breath caught in her throat, and for a minute he felt her hesitation, could almost hear her innermost thoughts. He pulled away, then looked down to her beautiful face and her amazing hazel eyes that were dark with a passion she probably had not experienced for ages.

This was a woman who had known so much heartache, had endured what appeared to be a loveless marriage.

Victor stared at her intently, his gaze shifting over her face. What was he thinking? she wondered.

Overcome with desire, Lillith pulled the shirt from Victor's pants and slid it up and over his broad shoulders. She knew she could have managed the movement with more grace, but her hands trembled and she felt a sense of urgency. She didn't want to think, only to feel, because Lord knew it had been far too long since she'd felt this way.

A low growl emanated from deep in Victor's throat, the sound exciting and primal, making her insides clench and her thoughts turn positively wanton.

Dark, silky hair caressed her cheek and she captured his beautiful face between her palms and kissed him. She could count only a handful of times she had been well and truly kissed by her husband, and she realized how very much she enjoyed it, the mingling of their breath, the stroke of his velvety tongue against her own.

Her hands moved down to his shoulders, then his upper arms, curling around his strong biceps. She felt so small and feminine beneath him. She wanted to be possessed fully by this man and savor his every touch.

His mouth left hers and made a pathway down her body, pressing a kiss along the rapidly beating pulse at her neck, at the slope of her breasts. His hands cupped the mounds, his thumbs brushing over her aching nipples, drawing them into tight buds. There seemed to be an invisible thread between her breasts and the flesh between her thighs.

He lowered his head and covered a nipple with his mouth, sucking it through the thin material of her chemise.

Liquid fire coursed through her veins, swooping low into her groin, making her insides tighten. Anticipation for what was to come raced through her.

One large, long-fingered hand moved downward, over her stomach, to the downy curls that covered her sex. Her thighs clamped tight together. He looked at her with a soft smile and reached for the hem of the chemise, drawing it farther up, over her thighs, toward her belly.

She stilled his movements with one hand. She was modest and was not sure she was ready for him to see her completely naked. What if he turned tail and ran? Her confidence could never overcome such a blow.

He let the chemise fall to her waist and continued his sexual play, kissing her nipples into agonizing, sensitive peaks before he slid down, his breath hot against her belly, his tongue grazing her navel, his lips pressing against the soft hair that covered her sex.

Her breath caught in her throat when she felt his hot breath fan her heated flesh. He licked her slit ever so slowly, the tip of his tongue teasing her clit.

Releasing a satisfied moan, she fisted his dark hair, holding him there, not daring to even breathe as his tongue danced over her flesh, bringing her body alive with each solid stroke.

Victor's cock was like stone against his belly, and he ached to be inside Lillith's hot, tight snatch. She was so sweet, and he could tell by the way she clung to him that she was very close to climax.

Every nerve in Lillith's body was alive with sensation. The buildup toward something wonderful had begun, and she felt closer to that pinnacle with every stroke of Victor's tongue against her dripping flesh.

His hands slipped beneath her buttocks, cupping her and bringing her closer to his face. The sweet pressure was too much to take, and when he sucked firmly on her tiny button, the dam broke, sending her reeling, her channel pulsing and throbbing with release. She bit her lip to keep from crying out and was shocked at the intense sensations rippling through her.

Desperate to feel him inside her, she tugged at the buttons of his trousers. His white teeth flashed as he looked at her, and he helped her unleash his impossibly hard cock.

He was exquisite—long and thick and every woman's dream. Her fingers wrapped around the impressive length, sliding up and down, reveling in the feel of velvet over steel.

Pulling the chemise from her, the sides of his mouth lifted as he stared at her breasts.

She had not felt this vulnerable in ages, and as he stared at her, she fought the gut reaction to pull the blanket up and over her.

"You're beautiful, Lily," he said, and she could tell by the look in his eyes that he meant it.

He bent his head and kissed a nipple, his cock bucking against her thigh.

She reached for him again, then opened her legs wider as she guided him to her slick entrance. The thick crown slid inside her, and she clenched her teeth as he pushed slowly, inch by inch, until he was imbedded fully inside her.

Victor was shocked at how tight she was—at the way her honeyed walls clamped around his length as snug as a glove.

Lillith moaned on a sigh, the feeling of being taken exquisite. His strokes were long and steady, each thrust bringing her closer to orgasm.

His lips were soft and gentle against hers; his tongue in rhythm with the movement of his lower body. He dipped his head to her neck, his tongue dancing at the place where her pulse pounded in an erratic beat.

He kissed the slope of her breasts, before taking a nipple into his mouth, licking the nub into a rigid peak.

Her nails dug into his back as heat coursed through her blood, and as he flexed his hips against her; his strokes fast and fluid, she cried out in pleasure as a powerful orgasm claimed her, sending her to the heavens.

Victor had never seen anything as beautiful as Lillith climaxing—her hazel eyes dark, heavy lidded; her mouth opening and a moan emanating from deep in her throat.

Her inner muscles throbbed around him, pulling him in deeper. She rotated her hips and that's all it took to push him over the edge, to an unforgettable orgasm that had him gasping for breath.

4

Lillith woke up in the middle of the night to a warm body beside her in bed.

A hard, muscled body.

She blinked a few times, pushing sleep away, and instantly became alert as she recalled the exquisite hours she'd spent making love to Victor Rayborne.

Her arm was tucked beneath his body, and it would be nearly impossible to ease it out from beneath him without waking him. Perhaps she *should* wake him. After all, she didn't want him slipping from her room in the morning when another guest might see him. With him wearing last evening's clothes, it would take little to figure out what he'd been doing and with whom.

Oh dear, what had she done? It was one thing to have a liaison behind the closed doors of one's own home, but to have a dalliance at a country home during a party was sheer stupidity.

Lillith tried to slide her hand out from beneath Victor, but the slight movement only made him nuzzle closer to her.

Her heart pounded in triple time as something else occurred

to her. What would she say when he woke up? She had never before experienced waking up with a lover at her side, and she could not remember a time in her marriage where Winfred had even lingered after sex.

Never had she felt so awkward. She eyed the chemise on the floor where Victor had thrown it hours earlier.

Victor sighed and nuzzled closer, his long hair brushing her cheek and bare shoulder. She breathed deeply of his wonderful earthy scent and fought the urge to bury her face in the dark curls.

He was everything she should avoid: a young, renowned rakehell with a sordid reputation for liking the wrong kind of women. He was a man who knew how to please, and he pleased her, giving her the first climax of her life, and that had been within minutes of him touching her.

Her stomach tightened at the memory of him tasting her, the sensation of his tongue sliding over her most intimate flesh, the way his fingers lifted her buttocks closer to his mouth, the heated look in his eyes as he'd glanced up at her while making delicious love to her.

And now the sheets barely covered his privates, showing the deep defined V that led to his sex. Her insides tightened instantly, knowing full well what lay beneath the covers. Slowly, her gaze moved up to his chiseled abdomen, to the wide chest, to the beautiful face.

His eyes fluttered opened and he looked right at her, the sides of his mouth slowly curving into a smile she felt all the way to her toes.

He was so lovely, and she had never wanted anyone so desperately.

"Come here, Lily," he said, pulling her into his arms, kissing her softly, and shocking her when he rolled so that she was on top of him.

Only once in her life had she attempted to take the reins in the bedchamber, and her husband had been less than receptive, his cock flaccid against his leg, his lips twisted in a mocking smile as she tried without success to excite him.

She had left his chamber horrified and her self-confidence shattered.

Those same vulnerabilities came rushing to the surface all over again—at least until Victor's hands moved up her sides and he braced her hips as he leveled her over his rock-hard cock.

She went to slide her hair over her breasts, but he would have none of it. He pushed the tresses over her shoulders. She swallowed hard as she sat down on him slowly, taking each inch inside her.

Rotating her hips, she smiled inwardly as he released a deep-throated moan, the sound purely male and so incredibly satisfying to her ego. Threads of pulsating desire threaded through her belly as she rode him, and she gained confidence with each steady stroke.

Falling into a steady rhythm, she let her head fall back on her shoulders, her nails digging into his chest as she rode him with wild abandon, listening to her body, and *her* needs.

Long, tapered fingers tightened on her hips, and Victor arched his hips off the bed, giving her every inch of his cock.

She could sense he was close to coming, but he held off, waiting for her. She looked down into his glittering eyes and the desire she saw in those blue depths took her breath away.

Victor palmed Lillith's firm breasts, his thumbs brushing over the small pink nipples, drawing them into tight buds. That simple touch was all that was needed to send her over the edge and splintering into a thousand pieces.

Lillith came with a groan, shifting her hips as wave after wave of pleasure rushed through her. Victor's low moans joined hers and she fell forward, her breathing ragged against his strong chest.

She heard the fast beat of his heart against her ear. His large hand moved up and down her spine, and she smiled as she slid off him and rolled onto her back.

She had never felt so sated.

He rolled onto his side, his large hand moving to her belly, settling there, his long fingers brushing along her rib cage, down over her navel, circling the small hollow cave.

Was this how it could be between two people? She had always hoped it could be, but to finally be experiencing it was almost overwhelming.

Going up on his elbow, he looked down at her and she stared at him, her throat tightening with an odd emotion. She found his good looks almost intimidating.

"Tell me about your marriage, Lily."

Her heart gave a jolt. What an odd question to ask someone after making love. Always, when it came to personal matters, she played her cards close to her chest, and the last thing she wanted to do was let her guard down.

She licked her lips and considered how much to divulge. "My marriage was not a happy time for me."

"Certainly you were happy at least part of the time?"

He looked and sounded skeptical. If only he knew the truth. If only everyone knew the truth of her marriage. "Early in my courtship, yes, I was happy because I was going to marry a man who I loved and respected, and I thought he felt likewise."

"That ended up not being the case?"

"Winfred played the part of doting fiancé well and had my entire family convinced he would treat me like a princess. I was madly in love with him and I thought he felt the same."

Victor played with her hair, his long fingers sliding through the tresses, putting her at ease and making her relax. "Did you sleep in the same bed?"

She had never before shared such intimate knowledge with

anyone but knew it was common for many married people, both happy and not, to not share a bed but rather retire to their own chambers each night. "No, we did not."

"Were the rumors true, then? Would he flaunt his lovers in front of you?"

She could not believe he had asked that specific question. Though she could deny it, she didn't. "Yes, he did. In fact, I think he took a perverse pleasure in seeing my pain."

"Bastard," he said, shaking his head. It felt strange to talk about her dead husband while in bed with another man, but Victor had a way of putting her at ease.

He threaded his fingers through hers, and she smiled when he kissed the back of her hand. "I'll never hurt you like that, Lily. I promise."

I'll never hurt you like that, Lily. I promise.

The words Victor had uttered to Lillith in the heat of the moment came back to haunt her the very next afternoon. While sitting in the parlor with a handful of guests, including Victor, Selene MacLeod walked into the room in a flourish of blue silk. She was Victor's mistress, or rumored mistress.

Good God, Lillith should have left while she had the chance.

It didn't help matters that Selene MacLeod was absolutely breathtaking with glossy dark hair and almond-shaped, light brown eyes. Scottish, she had a lovely and charming accent, but the most disturbing thing was that she was the exact opposite of Lillith in every possible way, not just in physical looks, but in the way she dressed and carried herself.

The woman's skin was flawless, not a single blemish or wrinkle. Diamonds dripped from her neck and throat, and her silk gown fit scandalously tight on her full breasts and slender waist.

And her legs went on forever.

She was tall, statuesque, and Lillith felt lacking in every possible way. Thoughts of her marriage came back to her in a rush as Victor, who had been sitting beside her chatting nonstop, went silent and stood.

Selene's eyes glittered with confidence as she approached Victor, who was quiet for the first time since Lillith had met him. Apparently, Selene had rendered him speechless.

"Bloody hell," Victor finally said under his breath.

From across the room, Lillith saw Rory and Sinjin approach, no doubt hoping to help ease the dreadful tension in the air. Lady Rochester looked taken aback by the woman's arrival, her color high as she stood back, letting her sons take the lead.

The women in the room were all aflutter in anticipation. Marilyn moved closer to Lillith, her hand sliding to her shoulder in silent commiseration.

Selene's gaze fell to Lillith for a few seconds. A finely arched brow lifted nearly to her hairline as a smirk played at her full lips.

Lillith's stomach tightened. She was not so stupid that she didn't know what that expression meant. She was laughing at her, sizing her up and finding her wanting. Everything within her screamed to walk away with her head held high, just as she had always done, but something also refused to back down and she stayed put. After all, Lillith had been invited, whereas Selene had not.

"What are you doing here, Selene?" Victor asked, his voice razor sharp.

"I came to see you, my darling," she said sweetly, flashing small, white teeth. "I have missed you since you left London. Imagine my dismay upon hearing you were throwing a country party and did not invite me."

"There is a reason you were not invited."

Her lips quirked. "Are you kicking me out, Vicky?" she asked, her voice challenging him.

"Miss MacLeod, the party is coming to an end, I am afraid," Sinjin said, intervening. "But you are always welcome to stay for dinner—and for the night, of course."

Victor's jaw clenched tightly.

Selene grinned. "Thank you, Lord Mawbry, for your kindness. I promise I shall be no trouble at all." Her gaze shifted to Rory, before returning to Victor. "You look well, Lord Graston."

His lips thinned. "As do you," he murmured.

Selene's gaze moved to Lillith again.

Lillith could feel her cheeks turn hot as the seconds ticked by. She could not wait to flee the room. In fact, she had half a mind to stay in her chamber until tomorrow morning, when she would return to London.

Selene put a hand on Victor's chest, the motion altogether too familiar and intimate in such a setting. Giggles filled the room, and Victor straightened and removed her hand. Lillith shook her head, shocked at how brazen the young woman was being, particularly in front of a crowd who waited breathlessly for her next move.

"She's scandalous," Marilyn said under her breath, while taking a seat beside Lillith.

"Are you packed for tomorrow?" Lillith asked, schooling her features.

Marilyn sat up straighter. "Yes, I am. In fact, I'm actually looking forward to London after spending a fortnight in the country."

Thank goodness for that. "I can appreciate the country, but I do not enjoy all the idle time," Lillith said almost absently. "I much prefer to be kept busy."

"I have no doubt we shall be very busy, Aunt Lily."

Lillith squeezed Marilyn's hand. "Yes, we have much to do. First and foremost, prepare for your coming out."

Marilyn nodded, "Indeed."

Victor and Selene slipped off to a corner, and Lillith refused to look at them, even though she would have given anything to hear the conversation. They spoke in low tones, and Victor kept shaking his head, clearly exasperated.

As the minutes wore on, Lillith found it difficult to keep her emotions in check, especially when Lady Rochester announced that dinner was ready and Selene slid her arm around Victor's. He had no choice but to escort her, and yet Lillith felt the sting of rejection heartily, especially when the two sat side by side.

Sitting at the head of the dinner table, Lady Rochester kept her eye on her middle son and his mistress. She made it very clear by her icy expression and demeanor that she was none too happy about the unexpected visitor, but there was not much she could do about it given Sinjin had invited her to stay.

Now they all had to get through the night, and Lillith wondered if Victor would come to her this evening, or if he would find his way to his mistress instead.

And what would she do or say if he did show up at her door tonight?

True, he had not invited the woman here, but still, the timing couldn't have been worse for Lilly and her newfound happiness.

Or perhaps it was a sign—a sign that she had been foolish and let her guard down, and now it was time to put it back up, return to life as she knew it, and remember this lesson for all eternity. After all, she was not a young, foolish girl any longer.

But she felt young and vulnerable.

And so very, very foolish.

"Lady Nordland, I understand you are interested in acquiring properties in London?" This came from Thomas Lehman, a handsome Irishman in his early thirties who had been openly pursuing Katelyn upon Lillith's arrival to the manor. Tall and with curly blond hair, he had garnered a lot of attention in the past week, but he had not singled a lady out.

She nodded, "Yes, as a matter of fact I am always on the lookout for properties. Sometimes I have them refurbished and sell them at a profit."

"I'm sure you do an incredible job of it too," he said with a wink. He was incredibly confident.

"Do you have a property in mind?"

"I do. I own a townhouse near St. James Square that is quite impressive. Perhaps when I return to London I can make an appointment to show it to you?"

She could feel someone watching her, and when she looked up Victor stared at her, his gaze shifting between herself and Thomas. Was he actually jealous? It seemed rather ridiculous given the fact his mistress, ex or otherwise, leaned into him, her huge breasts snug against his arm, her smile only for him.

Lillith pulled her gaze away. "Of course, Mr. Lehman. I would very much like to see the property you speak of. Thank you for thinking of me, and be sure to keep me in mind with any other properties or business ventures." She had added the last on a whim, more to irritate Victor than anything, but the Irishman looked absolutely elated.

Throughout dinner Thomas kept the conversation going, and Lillith was thankful for his company. It kept her focused on something other than the brooding young man sitting down the table and his witless mistress whose high-pitched laughter set Lillith's teeth on edge. Good God, did she have no sense of decorum?

"Would you take a walk with me about the gardens, Lady Nordland?" Thomas asked at the end of dinner. "It will do us both good to take the air in."

"Of course, Mr. Lehman," she replied, figuring why the hell not. She may as well enjoy a handsome young man's company, even if it wasn't the man she wanted. "Let me just check in with my nieces first."

Lillith spoke to both Katelyn and Marilyn before sliding her shawl over her shoulders. Mr. Lehman extended his arm and she slid her hand over his elbow and stepped outside. The wind had kicked up, but she welcomed the cool breeze against her heated cheeks. It had been a challenging day, one where she had experienced every depth of emotion possible.

This morning she had felt such excitement at the possibility of what could happen with Victor, and now she experienced nothing but bitter disappointment. All men were alike, but perhaps Victor had awakened in her a different woman—a sexual woman, one who was ready to take on a lover or two.

If she were discreet, perhaps she could —

"Are you ready to return home to London, Lady Nordland?" Thomas asked, his voice cordial and kind.

"Yes, Mr. Lehman, I am anxious, though I have made my primary home in Bath for some time. I enjoy the energy of London and all that it has to offer."

She had questioned Thomas's motives before, but honestly, he was not the only other man who had come to Claymoore Hall for the opportunity of meeting eligible young women. She knew little about him, but a few queries while in London should set her mind at ease.

"And I understand you are a patron of the arts."

He certainly had done his homework. She didn't know if she should be flattered or bothered by that. "I am, indeed. I very much enjoy creativity in all its forms; probably because I lack any such skill."

"I find that hard to believe, Lady Nordland. Your niece Marilyn says you have the voice of an angel."

She had been told she had a lovely voice on occasion, but she had not sung in public for many, many years, and she had no desire to do so. "My niece is far too kind."

"She also said you were humble, and I can tell she is right." He smiled boyishly, and Lillith could not help but return his kind smile. After a rather devastating night, he had taken her mind off Victor and made her feel special.

"Please, we have been talking only about me. Tell me of yourself, Mr. Lehman. I assume by your accent that you are Irish. Do you prefer England over your homeland?"

"I do. Like you, I favor London. The city is where I belong. I enjoy business, and I think I have a good mind for it."

"If that is so, I do indeed look forward to seeing this property you speak of," she murmured, and he beamed. She must tread carefully and not let herself be charmed by his smile and promise too much. She was known for her wise business ventures, and half the time she kept her thoughts unknown to the client, going solely through her solicitor.

She must be careful not to mix business and pleasure.

His blond hair was not far from the same shade as hers, and he had lovely, warm eyes. Lillith had always been attracted to dark haired men, and that had not changed in all these years.

They walked up the steps toward the verandah, and Lillith nearly missed a step upon seeing Victor standing against the balustrade, looking directly at her. He was with his brother Rory, and he was smoking. He inhaled deeply of the tobacco and lifted his chin, blowing a steady white stream into the cold air, not once looking away from her. Hell, he didn't even blink.

His blue eyes gave nothing away, and she wished she could read his mind. Rory said something to him and he nodded, finally glancing away. The two were as thick as thieves, the stories of their exploits common knowledge to everyone at the party.

What did they speak of now? she wondered.

As they came closer, Victor approached the steps. "May I have a word with you, Lady Nordland?" he asked, his tone cordial. He did not even glance at Thomas.

Lillith turned to her companion. "Mr. Lehman, thank you for a lovely evening. I so enjoyed your company."

Thomas brought her gloved hand to his lips and kissed her fingers gently. "The pleasure was all mine, Lady Nordland. I look forward to seeing you in London."

Lillith nodded and turned to Victor, whose jaw was clenched tightly. He waited until the door closed behind Thomas and Rory.

"I so enjoyed your company?" Victor said, the words flippant and curt.

By God, he *was* jealous.

5

Victor was furious. In fact, he didn't know who he wished to strangle more—Thomas or Lily.

Now he completely understood Sinjin's feelings when the other man had pursued Katelyn from the moment he'd set foot at Claymoore Hall.

He knew the Irishman was fucking Anna, because Rory had told him as much. Perhaps Lillith wouldn't be so keen to see him again if she knew that bit of information.

Lillith looked up at him, her hazel eyes innocent. "I did enjoy Thomas's company. He was very kind to me and treated me like a lady."

Meaning he hadn't?

Her lifted brow said as much.

Granted, pawing her beneath the table wasn't necessarily gentlemanly, but still, to be compared with Lehman and be left wanting was not a good feeling.

It hadn't helped matters that Selene had shown up unannounced.

"Where is your mistress?"

His hands clenched into fists at his sides. "She is not my mistress, Lillith."

Her lips quirked.

"Selene *was* my mistress, but I made it perfectly clear the last time we met that we were no longer involved."

"You owe me no explanation, Victor." The words were said with little inflection or emotion, and he wondered just how much she cared about him. Hell, maybe she didn't care, after all.

"I still wanted you to know that I did not expect Selene's arrival. Trust me when I say I wish she hadn't come."

"It means little to me."

The words cut to the quick. Probably more than they should have given they had slept together only one night.

He glanced at the tall windows where he could see the other guests mingling inside. God willing, his brothers would keep Selene busy.

Lillith released a frustrated sigh and started toward the double doors when he reached for her, his fingers encircling her wrist.

Tomorrow she would be leaving and he did not know when he would see her again, or if she even wanted to see him again. She glanced down at where he held her.

Taking her by the hand, he led her around the corner of the manor, off the pathway.

Lillith's eyes were wide as she looked around. They were alone, and no one would bother them here, save for someone walking down the garden pathway.

He stepped forward and she took a step back, and instantly felt her back come up against the stone, or rather, the manor walls. Victor leaned toward her, an arm on either side of her face, and kissed her, his lips not at all soft and gentle, but hard and demanding.

She wanted to resist him, but as much as her mind screamed

for her to push him away, her body would not cooperate. Instead, her arms slid around his strong neck and shoulders; her breasts smashed against his chest.

Cool air rushed up her legs, and it took her a moment to realize he was lifting her gown. She pulled her mouth from his to look at him, and she wished she wouldn't have. The look in his eyes was so sexual she knew she would never forget it, and knew that she could never tell him no.

He bent his head and kissed the slope of one breast, then the other. Pulling one globe from the tight confines, he kissed her nipple, teasing the rigid peak with the tip of his tongue and using his teeth with restraint. Butterflies fluttered in her stomach, and an intense ache grew between her thighs.

His gaze shifted to her lips; then he was kissing her again. With heart pounding nearly out of her chest, she gave in to her emotions and feelings.

Victor slid his hand between Lillith's thighs. She was so wet and hot for him. He slid a finger inside her, then kissed her breasts again before sliding another in her molten core; his thumb brushed her clit, flicking it until she was breathing hard.

Unbuttoning his trousers, desperate to touch him, she unleashed his cock. Her fingers slid over the length, squeezing him tight in her fist.

She worked with a practiced skill that had Victor clenching his teeth. If she did not stop soon, he would spend himself, and that would not do.

He slid inside her snug cunny and they moaned in unison.

His strokes were short and fluid, and Lillith clung to him as liquid fire rushed through her veins, settling in the place where their bodies joined.

He cupped his hips tight against her, causing an exquisite friction. Lillith wrapped her legs around him, taking him farther into her body, shifting her hips, moaning with ecstasy.

His cock swelled inside her channel, and he slowed his pace, the plum-sized crown slipping out just enough to make her follow him, her hips arching. She swallowed a groan as he filled her again.

Lillith's nails dug into his shoulders, and he barely had to move because she was soon riding him, her pace faster and faster. He tightened his grip on her bottom, and was relieved when he heard her moan and felt her sheath tighten and pulse around his cock.

He held on long enough to let her finish, and with a few solid thrusts, met his own completion.

Victor released her and Lillith slid to her feet, and instantly yanked her skirts down. What on earth had made her lose all sense of self and rut like a whore outside the manor, where anyone could have come upon them? She looked around. They had been up against the manor, so no one could see them from the house—even from a window, save perhaps for a person sticking his head out. But given the cool air and the fact that the majority of the guests were still in the parlor or dining area, she hoped that would not be the case.

"Please don't leave tomorrow," he whispered, kissing her again. He confused her, and she didn't like the way she was beginning to feel. For so long she had put up a wall to guard her feelings, and he was beginning to chip away at that wall, slowly but surely.

Which meant she had to leave before she made a mistake—like make love outside in the open and ruin her long-standing reputation. What a scandal it would be if the *ton* learned of her little tryst with the young lord.

Her conscience wanted to say, *the hell with it,* especially when men could marry or have mistresses half their age, but women were not allowed the same luxury as men. Look at Loraine and her young lover. She was the talk of London. Many laughed at her, but Lillith also knew that the ones doing the whispering were unhappy women who were married to old men who did not love or appreciate them. In truth, they probably secretly envied Loraine.

"Lily, will you stay?" Victor asked, lifting her chin with strong fingers.

"Victor?" she heard a woman's voice call out, and Lillith sucked in a breath. It was Selene, and she was coming their way. The last thing she wanted or needed was Selene finding her alone with Victor.

Victor sighed and Lillith pulled away from him, rushing along the grass toward the back of the manor, away from Selene and the other guests.

Rory walked into the dimly lit room, stunned to find Lady Anna was not alone.

Thomas Lehman stood, naked as the day he'd been born, hands on hips, watching Anna as she undressed.

Apparently he had not received the news that their tête-à-tête had been rescheduled. He slowly backed out of the room, but Anna caught his movement. "Rory—we've been waiting for you!"

We've? He eased a finger between his suddenly too-tight cravat and throat. Certainly he'd shared women before, but always with his brothers, namely, Victor. The rules had been very simple: Share, but always respect the other person's boundaries. "Um, perhaps another night."

"I'm leaving tomorrow," Anna blurted, walking toward him. She wore a cream-colored silk night rail that revealed far more than it hid, and his body had taken notice, or more importantly, his cock had taken notice.

"Anna, I . . ." he began, but she placed a slender finger on his lips.

"Come, Rory. You'll enjoy it. I promise."

He could not even look at Thomas.

"Actually, we're both leaving tomorrow. You will not have to see us after tonight—that is, if you don't wish to." The news they were both leaving wasn't entirely surprising, and a part of him was actually glad . . . especially if he did join in on the ménage à trois.

A thousand reasons why he should leave raced through his mind, and yet when Anna's hand slid down his, taking his hand in hers, he did not pull away.

She led Rory toward Thomas. The other man started stroking his cock, and Rory dropped his gaze to the floor between them. He considered himself to be sexually adventurous, but this was even a bit too much for him. He jerked away and shook his head. "I don't think—"

"Come, don't be shy," Anna said, a sly smile on her lips as she all but pulled his jacket from him, following with his waistcoat. She tossed both items aside, ripped the shirt from his trousers, and slid it up and over his head before he could blink. She definitely wasn't going to give him time to back out.

Next, she unbuttoned his trousers, her agile fingers sliding around the base of his cock and sliding slowly upward. She quickly worked him into a satisfactory state of arousal.

"Sit in the chair, Thomas," she said over her shoulder, her voice downright demanding, and the Irishman did what she said, cock standing at attention.

She took Rory by the hand and led him over toward Thomas. Rory slid the flimsy night rail up and over her head, letting it fall to the floor at their feet.

He played with her breasts, and she leaned back against him. Thomas slid his fingers between her thighs, and soon she was rocking against Rory, her head resting against his shoulder.

She placed a hand on Thomas's wrist and pushed his hand

away. Rory knew how she liked to prolong the ecstasy and took pleasure in the waiting.

She straddled Thomas and slid onto his cock, her back arched, her bottom sticking out. She had a lovely back, her bottom pert and lush.

Anna turned and worked Rory's erection, her slender fingers sliding up and down the length. He wasn't as hard as usual, no doubt given the unusual circumstance, so he closed his eyes until she pulled him toward her and took him inside her hot mouth.

If there was one thing he could say about Anna, it was she had a delectable mouth and knew how to use it. Rory cupped his hips as she took him expertly, her tongue laving the head, before sliding down and over him again and again, sucking him hard until his cock responded in kind.

"Take me from behind," she whispered, and he opened his eyes. Thomas was watching him, a strange heated look in his brown eyes. Having never tried anal sex, Rory's heart missed a beat as excitement rippled along his spine. He swallowed past the lump in his throat and positioned himself behind Anna—between Thomas's spread thighs.

Trying to ignore the feeling of hard, muscled legs pressed firmly against his own, he slowly slid the crown of his cock into her rectum, past the tight ring of muscle there. She didn't move, nor did Thomas as he sank into her, inch by inch. He gritted his teeth. She was so incredibly tight, no doubt more so because the other man's cock was buried deep inside her. He knew just the slightest hint of skin separated his cock from the other man's, and it made him uneasy.

But not so uneasy he was about to stop.

Anna moaned when he was all the way in.

"Fuck me," Anna said, to which one of them he didn't know, but he started to move, and so did Thomas. Soon the three broke into a rhythm that had Rory quickly reaching for what would be an unforgettable climax. Thomas was getting close, too, and it bothered him that the man looked directly at him and not at Anna. Rory concentrated on the back of Anna's head, and finally just closed his eyes.

Minutes later, Thomas let out a guttural moan, his breathing labored as he pulled out of Anna, his semen shooting onto her flat stomach.

Rory could feel Anna's tight inner muscles clamp as she came. He pumped a few more times and filled her back passage with semen, flexing his hips against her ass. His legs nearly buckled as the final pulses rippled through him.

He slid from her and immediately stepped away from the two. He was still trembling when he reached for his shirt. All the while Thomas sat in the chair watching him. Anna wiped her stomach with the night rail and walked over to her bed and lay down with an exaggerated sigh. "I wish I could take you both home with me," she said, biting her bottom lip as she looked at Rory, who now had his shirt and waistcoat on and was slipping back into his jacket.

Thomas had yet to move from the chair.

"So you're leaving in the morning?" Rory asked, more out of politeness than general curiosity.

"Yes, I'll look you up soon enough, though. I hope to visit friends in London within a fortnight. Perhaps I shall see you then?"

"Perhaps the three of us can get together again?" Thomas said eagerly.

"Perhaps," Rory said, already walking toward the door. This was one liaison he wouldn't be talking about anytime soon.

* * *

Victor watched the carriage pull away from the manor, his gut sinking further into his stomach.

He knew Lillith was leaving today, so it wasn't a huge surprise when he saw her outside, sitting beside a tower of baggage, awaiting the carriage.

Apparently someone was anxious to get home.

He tried not to let his ego be slighted in any way because she was ready to flee Claymoore Hall, especially after their tryst in the garden last night after Selene's sudden arrival.

He had no intention of throwing up her skirts and fucking her like he would any common whore, but a combination of desire and jealousy had gotten the best of him, and the moment had been intense and exciting.

Last night he could sense her embarrassment when Selene had called out to him right after the interlude. Her timing had been horrible, and had he a few more minutes alone with Lillith, she would perhaps be staying on at Claymoore Hall. But Lillith had rushed off and he had answered Selene, all the while hoping she hadn't seen Lillith retreat.

Later, when the house had quieted down, he had gone to Lillith's room, but she had not answered, and he had not risked waking others by pounding on her door, but how he'd wanted inside her chamber.

Though a part of him wanted to say he was relieved she was leaving, the fact of the matter was he had enjoyed making love to Lillith. It had been extremely gratifying in a way that shocked him. True, he'd had a good number of mistresses in his twenty-nine years, but not a single one who had made him consider marriage. Not a single one he'd wanted to introduce to his parents.

And oddly, while Lillith had been beneath him, sighing and moaning, her lithe body meeting him thrust for thrust, he had a flash of what life could be like with just one woman—a beautiful, loyal, and trustworthy woman at that.

A woman like Lillith.

Selene slid her hand to his hip. Last night she had come to his chamber and he had promptly sent her away, telling her in no uncertain terms that they would not be taking up where they had left off. He still remembered the night he'd discovered she'd been fucking the count behind his back. The betrayal had hurt immensely.

Like now, even after his refusal, she tried to use her feminine charms to change his mind, but he was not having it. No, he wanted to be with Lillith.

"Your widow has left you, I see," Selene said. Her voice hinted at humor, though her expression was all sympathy. She was a good actress, after all.

"She must return to London."

The corner of her lips curved the slightest bit. "And will you return to London, Victor?"

"I will."

"Will you visit me?"

It was a bold request given that the count kept her in elaborate style in the fashionable Mayfair District of London. "At your lover's townhouse? I think not, Selene."

"Are you jealous?" She actually sounded hopeful.

Initially upon hearing the news, Victor had been jealous; but truth be told, that jealousy had faded with time, each day easier than the one before. In fact, when Selene had walked into Claymoore Hall, the vast disappointment he had felt had been palpable. "No, Selene, I am not jealous."

As Lillith's carriage turned the final corner out of Claymoore Hall and disappeared, Victor felt her absence like a punch to the gut. The manor held no appeal for him now that she was gone. Poor Sinjin, he thought, his gaze falling on his brother who stood out on the front steps, hands on hips. His bride-to-be was in that carriage, so he was suffering more so than Victor. No doubt he yearned to be done with the party once and for all, and return to London as soon as possible.

If it weren't for Balliford's suicide, he would have married Katelyn immediately, but his mother had told him that waiting at least five or six months would be the proper thing to do. Society would be more accepting of the union that way too.

Selene let her hand fall away from him. "You would tire of her anyway, Victor. She is not the type of woman who could keep you satisfied."

"How do you know that I would tire of her? You know nothing about Lily."

He could see the surprise in her eyes. "Well, I know enough. She is not your type. Rest assured she would bore you by week's end."

"I doubt that," he said, running his hands through his hair. "Were you not leaving today?"

She flinched as though he'd struck her. "I had considered leaving, but if you would like me to stay—"

"I think you should go."

He had not meant to be so abrupt, but he really was in a foul mood and wanted her gone.

Her eyes narrowed. "You might enjoy the hunt, Victor, but you wait and see—in time you will grow weary of the chase with your little widow, and you'll want to get on to marrying someone who is young enough to give you lots of children."

"Lillith has many years of childbearing left."

"You are *actually* considering marriage?" She didn't even try to hide her disbelief.

"I didn't say that, Selene, but to Lady Nordland's credit, she has all the qualities a man would want in a woman. She has proven herself to be kind, courteous, and above all, *loyal.*" He said the last with an edge.

"I was loyal to you, Victor."

"And you are a fantastic liar."

"I never lied to you."

"Tell that to your count. Perhaps he will believe you."

"I was not unfaithful."

He laughed without mirth. "From the time we got together I heard stories about who you were fucking behind my back, but I chose to ignore them, believing the rumors came from mere jealousy. I can tolerate infidelity from a mistress, but never from a wife."

Her chin lifted high. "If we were to marry, I would be loyal to you." She took his hand in hers, her fingers curling around his. Going up on the tips of her toes, she kissed him, her lips firm, trying hard to coax a response. "I swear it, Victor. If you marry me, I shall make you the happiest man alive," she whispered, her hand moving to the buttons of his trousers.

He stilled her hand, his fingers curling around her wrist. "Go home to your count, Selene. What we had is over."

"You cannot mean that. What we had together was beautiful. I love you, Victor."

"You don't know what love is." He released her hand and without another word, walked away, ignoring the sounds of her sobs.

6

The rain pelted hard against the windows, and Lillith pulled her shawl tight about her shoulders. The weather had been dreadful since her return to London, so she had stayed close to home rather than venture out.

Across the street, a finely dressed couple rushed up the steps. Lillith smiled to herself. Her new neighbors were newlyweds who had been given the townhouse as a wedding present from the groom's excited parents. She remembered well the feelings of being a newlywed, so in love and so unaware of what the real world was all about.

The young bride had visited Lillith just yesterday, dropping by with a bouquet of fresh roses to welcome her back to London. It had been a lovely gesture, and Lillith had been delighted that both Katelyn and Marilyn had been there to meet the young woman, who hopefully would become a good friend to both her nieces.

As the two entered the townhouse, Lillith let the drape slide back into place.

Truth be told, the weather was not the only reason she

stayed close to home. She had little desire to be in public and put on a happy face, especially when she was miserable, not to mention mad at herself for having given in to her desires. She did not regret meeting Victor, but she regretted getting romantically involved with him. If she had just resisted and not slept with him, then she would not be experiencing pain now. It was that simple.

And though she tried to tell herself that leaving Claymoore Hall without saying anything to Victor had been the right thing to do, she knew deep in her heart it had been wrong. How would she have felt if the tables had been turned? They had been overtaken by their desire and made love out in the open. Just because she was angry at her own behavior, didn't mean she should take it out on him, and yet she had.

Edward opened the door and she turned to him. "Yes, Edward."

"A Mrs. Rencourt is calling."

Lillith's eyes widened.

A week ago, when Lillith had returned to London, she had written her old friend in a moment of whimsy. Janet brought back memories of long-forgotten summers playing in meadows and climbing trees, and visiting market with their parents.

Like herself, Janet had married at a young age, and to a man a good deal older than herself. Apparently her husband's stamina was no match for hers and she'd immediately taken a lover, and her reputation had been sullied forever.

It was shameful to say, but soon thereafter Lillith had distanced herself from her friend, despite Janet's frequent attempts to be part of her life.

She had not agreed with her friend's lifestyle and, quite frankly, had not wanted to associate herself with a woman who had become so brazen. It had been too stark a reminder that her husband was unfaithful.

And yet, on the ride from Claymoore Hall to London, her friend's face kept popping into her mind, along with all the happy times they had experienced together as girls and young women.

Edward cleared his throat. "Should I show her up, my lady?"

"I'm so sorry, Edward. Yes, of course."

Lillith sat in the chair beside the fire and smoothed out her skirts.

"Mrs. Rencourt," Edward said.

Lillith stood as her old friend swept into the room, looking extremely youthful and full of life.

Janet's wide smile put Lillith at ease, and a sense of remorse came over her as she remembered the curt nods she had given her friend at the opera or rare soiree they might have both been attending.

"Could you please bring us tea, Edward?" Lillith asked.

"Right away, my lady." Edward backed out of the room, closing the door behind him.

Janet's lithe form was outfitted in a lovely day dress of ivory with blue roses, the colors complementing her auburn hair that had been arranged in full curls, held in place by a navy demi-turban of fine muslin.

Her friend had mothered two children: a boy who had gone into the navy, and a girl who had married a man three times her age and lived in the Austrian Alps. Rumor had it Janet would be a grandmother very soon.

"Janet, you look wonderful."

Janet grinned, her white teeth flashing. "As do you, my dearest, Lillith. I cannot tell you how happy I was to hear from you after all these years."

Embarrassed by her past behavior, Lillith smiled. "I am glad that you are here now. How have you been?"

Janet set back in her chair, her head tilting to the side. "Very well, thank you. But what of you? I was stunned to hear of Lord Balliford's death."

"Indeed, it was stunning," Lillith said, wondering what her friend would think if she knew the whole truth behind Lord Balliford's demise. To save his family and Katelyn from embarrassment, the family told the general public that Balliford's and his sister's deaths were caused by a freak accident. Lillith had seen the terrifying events unfold for herself, and that horrible day would stay with her for the rest of her life. "As you have probably heard, Katelyn is now engaged to Lord Mawbry."

"Indeed, I have," Janet said, her eyes lighting up. "Such a handsome man, as are all the Rayborne men. I attended a soiree one evening where all three were in attendance, and my goodness, the women were all aflutter." Lillith's stomach twisted. "Indeed, they are all very handsome and draw attention wherever they go. Katelyn is a very lucky girl."

"Yes, she is, but so is Sinjin to have her," Lillith said with a wink. "I think the two will get along very well."

"I am sure you are right," Janet said in a lighthearted tone. "Tell me, did Sinjin's brothers find any of the young debutantes to their liking?"

To Lillith's dismay, she felt herself blush and hoped that Janet did not guess the cause. "I do not know, to be honest. I did not notice them singling any one woman out."

"Their mother must be happy that at least one of them found a bride."

"I am sure she is." Lillith had a feeling Lady Rochester would not relent until all her sons were married.

"Are your nieces staying with you for the rest of the summer, then?"

Lillith dropped her gaze. Loraine had insisted the girls stay with her "while things calmed down" after Lord Balliford's death and Katelyn's sudden engagement to Sinjin. "They have gone to stay with their mother for a while."

"Ah, how is Loraine?"

"Well, thank you."

"I was always surprised how very different you and your sister are."

"Indeed, we are."

Janet must have sensed that Lillith did not wish to speak about Loraine, because she said, "Tell me what you have been up to. I have missed you immensely, Lily."

The words struck at Lillith's heart and made her throat tighten. She had missed Janet too. She'd never had another friend like her in all these years. To think that they could very well start over made her extremely happy. "I have missed you too. I have not been a very good friend to you over the years, Janet, and I am sorry for that."

Janet looked down at her gloved hands and smiled. Obviously she wasn't going to refute the statement.

"The past is just that. There is no sense in crying over what cannot be changed."

Lillith was relieved. "So . . . you never remarried?"

"Good Lord, no. I confess I like my freedom far too much to be tied down to any man."

Lillith nodded and smiled, her earlier nervousness fleeing.

"And what of you, Lily?" she said, leaning close, lowering her voice. "You've been alone for a while. Have you taken a lover?"

Nearly choking, Lillith blushed and shook her head. She could tell Janet the truth, but she was not certain she wanted anyone to know about Victor. What they had shared had been so wonderful, and she wanted to keep the memory to herself. "No."

She looked surprised. "Why would you deny yourself the one freedom us widows have?"

Lillith shrugged. "I have been too busy."

"Oh, fiddle-faddle. One is never too busy for sex. In fact, remaining sexual is good for one's health and one's peace of mind. I would never deny myself that luxury, and you should do the same. You are beautiful, Lily, and your body is unravaged from childbirth."

Lillith knew her friend did not make the comment about not having children to hurt her, but to instead pay a compliment, but the fact that she had never been a mother still stung, especially since she had desperately wanted children of her own.

"Do not get me wrong—I love my children, but my body has never been the same since having them."

"I would have traded my body for children at any time during my marriage," Lillith said, meaning it.

Janet rolled her eyes. "Spoken like a woman who has never known the hardships of motherhood."

Lillith smiled to herself, knowing full well her old friend was an excellent mother, and both children had gone on to do great things with their lives. "You have lovers, then?"

Janet's grin widened. "Of course. I am seeing several different men at the moment."

"Several?" The word came out a croak.

She nodded. "Indeed, one of the men I am seeing is Lord Dench."

Lillith flinched. The man was a widower of advanced years and was known to have a horrendous gambling habit.

"Alex treats me very well and spoils me beyond reason. He hates that I have other lovers, but I told him I would never be exclusive."

"And what of your other lovers?" Lillith asked, wondering if she should push for an answer. Being privy to such information might make her uncomfortable, and yet she was curious. "Have you ever had a man who is younger than yourself?"

Janet's eyes lit up. "Oh yes, I have to say that, although I do not necessarily enjoy a younger man's company outside the bedchamber, I do enjoy the enthusiasm shown *inside* the bedchamber. Usually their stamina is incredible. You really must try it."

"Why do you not enjoy them outside the bedchamber?"

"I have found younger men to be ever so dull when it comes to conversing. Normally they wish to talk about themselves incessantly." Janet cleared her throat, then glanced toward the doors through which the valet had left.

"If you are interested, I could introduce you to a number of young men who you could entertain without concern of having to reveal your identity."

"I do not understand. How could I *entertain* a man without revealing my identity?"

Janet leaned close. "I am a member in a very exclusive club; one that I think you might enjoy."

Her stomach tightened. "Like a gentleman's club?"

"It is an exclusive hideaway where keeping one's identity is top priority. The members pay a hefty sum in order to belong, and understand that breaking the rules will result in punishment of a most unpleasant nature."

"Do you mean people have sex at this place?"

Janet smiled coyly. "Indeed."

Lillith's eyes widened. Certainly she had heard of such places before but had never imagined any one of her friends would be involved in any way. "Has anyone ever broken the rules?"

"Not that I know of. Honestly, I do not know why anyone would. It is so much fun, Lillith. The anonymity makes it even more titillating."

"You do not know who you are making love to?" she whispered, not wanting her staff to overhear her.

"No, everyone wears masks, and normally wigs, too, in order to keep their identity from being revealed. The first time I ever attended such an event I was insecure, but my good friend assured me that my identity would be kept a secret, and I fully enjoyed myself. I am a member in good standing and I attend as often as I can. I have never regretted my decision."

"Do your current lovers know about this place, this hideaway?"

"For all I know they might very well be members, though I doubt it. I highly recommend attending—at least once, my dearest Lily. You can have sex with as many people as you want, and no one will judge you. No names are used, and no faces; just two people, or more, coming together to experience mutual satisfaction."

The very idea of having sex with a person whose face you couldn't see was hardly appealing.

"It is incredibly exhilarating to be taken by a man you have never met before."

Lillith flinched. Making love to someone you'd never met before sounded dirty and wrong.

"In all honesty, I have had three lovers at one time. It was a most gratifying experience."

Lillith frowned. "Three lovers at one time? How is that possible without someone standing around watching?"

Janet licked her lips and gave a saucy wink. "My dearest, Lily, we were all occupied, I assure you."

Lillith's cheeks flushed as scandalous images flashed in her mind.

"Truth be told, I could not stand for days after, but what wonderful memories," Janet said, sounding extremely gratified.

"I do not think that would be a place for me. I would be extremely uncomfortable."

"I think it is exactly the kind of place for you, Lily. What have you ever done for yourself, save for being a good wife to a man who did not appreciate you." Janet reached out and took hold of her hand. "I have heard the stories, Lily. I know all about Winfred and his male lovers—and the horrific way you were treated during your marriage. I do so wish I could have been in your life to help ease your pain."

Of course she knew that all of London had heard the cruel truth about her marriage, but it was still difficult to hear it, especially from her friend.

"And that is why now I want you to experience the ecstasy of the hideaway for yourself. Of course I will not leave your side the entire night, I promise. Well, unless you ask me to."

A knock at the door made Lillith jump, and Janet took a sip of tea and sat back in her chair.

Edward appeared at the door with tea. "Tea and scones, my lady," he said, walking toward them.

"That would be lovely," Lillith replied, hoping he had not overheard any of their conversation.

Janet gave Edward a lazy glance, and the valet shifted beneath her obvious stare. Edward had worked for Lillith for the past ten years. At least fifteen years her senior and married to the cook, Lillith could not remember a time anyone had paid him any extra interest.

"Mrs. Rencourt," he said, filling Janet's cup. Her friend did not once drop her gaze, and the poor valet nearly overfilled the tea cup before catching himself. By the time he served Lillith, his cheeks were bright red, and he couldn't get out of the room fast enough.

Janet watched his departure with lifted brow. When she met

Lillith's gaze, they grinned, and for the first time in a long while Lillith laughed, and it felt wonderful.

"So what do you say, Lily? Will you go with me to the hideaway next time I go?"

Lillith could hear her heart pound in her ears. "I do not know, Janet. I just don't believe I would be comfortable. And what if someone recognized me?"

"No one will recognize you."

"But what if they did?"

"They would hope that you did not recognize them in turn, and know that because of the circumstances, you will never reveal their identity to anyone." She added a large dollop of clotted cream to her scone before taking a bite. "Plus, just because you are visiting does not mean you have to participate."

"You are not obligated to do so?" Lillith asked, genuinely surprised.

"Of course not. Many people enjoy watching. You might find that is enough for you."

7

How had no ended up being yes? Lillith wondered, sitting across from Janet in the black, nondescript carriage that had picked them up some thirty minutes before.

Janet grinned widely, her teeth flashing white in the dark interior. "Relax, my dear, you will have the time of your life."

There was not a chance in Hades she would ever relax. How had she allowed herself to be talked into attending such an event at the hideaway, or what Janet had laughingly called the "den of iniquity."

Janet handed her the silver flask she'd been drinking from all evening. Was she nervous as well, Lillith wondered, taking the flask and bringing it to her lips. The whiskey burned her mouth, all the way down her throat, but she welcomed the warmth. She needed to ease the fear racing through her; a difficult thing to do when everything within her said to tell the driver to turn the carriage around. "What if someone recognizes us?"

"We have been through this, Lily," Janet said, doing her best not to show her exasperation, but Lillith could sense it in her voice. "The carriage is rented, the drivers too. Your identity is safe, so quit fretting. Soon we shall arrive and you will wonder why you have made such a fuss."

"What of my nieces or my sister? What if they were to discover—"

"They will be none the wiser. In fact, *no one* will be the wiser, and truth be told, I would be stunned if Loraine has not attended such an event herself."

She could very well be right.

Lillith had no time to think on it, for the carriage rolled to a stop and Lillith's stomach clenched tight. The coach shifted as the driver stepped down from his perch, then the door was opening, the cool air hitting her full in the face. "Oh dear, I think I might be sick."

"Do not be so melodramatic," Janet said, excitement tingeing her voice. "You shall have the time of your life, and no one will have an inkling of who you are."

Dressed in an outrageous scarlet gown with a red wig and a velvet black mask that covered the better part of her face, Lillith hoped Janet was right and she would be safe from discovery.

"Oh, and no one speaks either."

"Then how do you communicate?"

Janet's lips curved into a wicked smile. "Sometimes words are not needed, my dear."

Despite the coolness of the evening, Lillith whipped open her fan and began waving it before her flushed cheeks. "But what about . . . limits? What if you need to say no?"

Janet shook her head. "A single nod or shake of the head is all that is required."

Lillith felt like such an amateur.

The driver reached up to help Janet down, and then Lillith. Though a black curtain had kept her ignorant of her surroundings, she was aware they were definitely no longer in London, which made sense. They had been traveling for a good forty minutes. For all she knew they could have been circling the block any number of times, and yet the building they were at now sat alone on a few acres, hidden by towering oak trees and a high hedge that ran the perimeter of the property.

They were most definitely not in London any longer.

"What if I decide I wish to leave?" Lillith asked, spying a row of horse and carriages. Ironically, each driver was dressed in black from head to toe. Apparently these individuals took discretion seriously.

"We shall stay an hour at least, and if you decide after such a time you wish to leave, then we will go. How does that sound?" Janet asked.

Although it had been decades since last they had done anything together, Lillith chose to take her word for it that Janet would leave if she so wished.

"Likewise, if you find you are having a lovely time and wish to be left alone with a gentleman, just let me know. I will wait for you."

Lillith was here because Janet had pushed her to come, and because there was a certain part of her that was curious as to how the other half lived. Perhaps now that she had made love to Victor, she would be more apt to explore her sexuality. And this was as good a place to start as any, and with people who had no idea who she was.

A tall black man with a white powdered wig opened the heavy double doors, and they entered the dimly lit foyer that was surprisingly silent.

Lillith's heart pounded hard as they walked through an archway and past another man, this one dressed similarly to the first. He pointed down the long, narrow hallway with dark wood paneling. Gold sconces lit their way, and the smell of incense was increasingly stronger the farther they walked. She heard the soft strains of stringed instruments.

She stopped for a moment and glanced back over her shoulder.

"Ready?" Janet whispered, excitement flashing in her eyes as she took Lillith's hand and led her toward a large, red velvet drape.

Lillith nodded, and taking a deep breath, she stepped into the room.

The space was as large as the parlor in her townhouse, bright red with mahogany wainscoting coming halfway up the wall. More thick velvet drapes separated several areas of the rooms, and Lillith wondered what happened behind that covering.

Musicians, hidden behind sheer draperies, played for the crowd, effectively keeping identities secure. Lillith imagined, given the secretive nature of the event, they must be paid a hefty sum.

"Ladies, would you care for wine?" a woman dressed in a medieval milkmaid costume asked.

Janet took two glasses and handed one to Lillith. Her friend touched her glass to hers and took a sip. Lillith refrained from drinking, terrified there was something more than alcohol in the glass.

As they weaved their way through the crowd, Lillith found the lack of conversation a bit disconcerting. Still, despite the rule of no talking, there was a lot of touching, smiling, and batting of eyelashes going on.

It was an interesting play between the sexes—strange and titillating all at the same time. She scanned the crowd, looking at the array of costumes. Surprisingly, there were couples who were dressed alike, one Caesar and Cleopatra. The woman's black wig and thick makeup the only thing hiding her identity from others.

Lillith saw a man dressed in a dark green frockcoat and a tricorn hat. His back was to her, but he had nice broad shoulders, a narrow waist, and strong legs. His mask was a black silk sash tied at the back of his head, with small slits for his eyes. He made a dashing highwayman.

A shiver rushed along her spine as she imagined Victor dressed in such a costume. Her heart squeezed as she remembered their last night together, the passion between them. She wished she could read his mind and know what he truly felt about her.

What would he think if he could see her now in such a place? True, she had not seen anything remotely scandalous yet, but the night was young.

The highwayman turned abruptly and his eyes scanned the room. Her pulse skittered when his gaze stopped on her, and the sides of his mouth lifted in a smile.

She quickly looked away but could feel his stare continue to burn into her, daring her to look away.

"Goodness me, you have an interested party," Janet whispered behind her fan.

Not wanting to say a word for fear of someone recognizing her voice, Lillith took a sip of wine. The room was growing warmer by the second and her borrowed gown too tight.

She touched her neck, feeling the wig, making sure it had not slipped to reveal her blond hair.

All in the room had gone to great lengths to hide their identity, and although Lillith knew secrecy was the order of the day, she could not help but feel guilty at being in such a place.

In the far corner, behind a thick burgundy curtain, suspicious grunts could be heard. Lillith took a step back and glanced over. She could see the back of a masked man, his hips moving in a steady, familiar rhythm. Her stomach clenched. Good gracious, was he making love to someone right here?

"Come, I want to show you something," Janet said, taking her by the hand. Lillith gave the highwayman one last glance before they walked out.

They went into a hallway, then up a set of stairs. Off the landing there were doorways in both directions, and to Lillith's surprise, Janet went straight for the second door to the right. They slipped in, and Janet closed the door tightly behind them and locked it. The room was small, and had a settee and two large chairs. Janet went to the wall and took off the painting, where there were two holes in the wall.

Lillith wasn't so naive that she didn't realize what the holes were for.

"There are those who enjoy watching other people make love, and who, in turn, find being watched an aphrodisiac. Do you wish to watch a couple make love, Lily?" Janet asked, sitting in one of the large chairs.

Lillith stepped to the wall and looked into the room. There was a four-poster bed in the center covered by a black silk coverlet. At the four corners were red silk ties, and the room was lit by candelabras on either side of the bed.

"It is empty."

"Trust me, it will not be for long. Sit, and drink with me. Tell me what you think so far."

Lillith sat down, for the first time really taking a look at the artwork in the room. Naked women laying in varying poses lined one wall, and a crystal bowl on a side table was full of condoms. "It is interesting. I cannot get used to the lack of talking. It seems odd to have so many people in one place and no voices, just the occasional whisper."

She nodded and set her glass aside. "Perhaps you and the highwayman will—"

The door to the opposite room opened, and Janet bit her lip and pointed toward the wall.

Lillith felt strange as she peeked into the room. It was the woman dressed as Cleopatra, her generous curves draped in a white flowing gown that clung to her hips and ample breasts. Lillith fully expected the man dressed as Caesar to follow her in, but instead it was the highwayman.

Janet looked at her and lifted a brow, clearly as surprised as she was.

The man removed his hat, stripped off his coat and tossed it over a chair, and then started to remove his shirt. Lillith's breath caught in her throat when he looked in her direction.

"He does not know it is us," Janet whispered reassuringly, but Lillith wondered. Certainly with the size of the establishment there were rooms aplenty. She could be in any one of the rooms, so it was impossible he would know it was her, she told herself.

The man, with the help of his companion, removed his boots and unbuttoned his breeches, sliding them down his long legs, then kicking them aside.

His cock jutted from a nest of light brown curls. The dark wig remained on his head, as did the mask. The woman smiled appreciatively, her hand gripping his cock and kneading his length that grew with her efforts.

"Oh my," Lillith said under her breath, and Janet laughed quietly.

The highwayman helped his companion off with her dress and flung it aside, managing all along to keep his mask, and hers, in place.

With a fierce growl, he lifted the woman in his arms and

tossed her onto the bed roughly, a devilish smile on his face as he took great care in tying each limb to a bed post. The woman was facedown in the silk sheets, plump butt in the air as she wriggled in anticipation. The highwayman made sure to give enough play in the binds so that his lover could still move her arms and legs.

Lillith's stomach tightened and excitement rushed through her veins as she waited. What would it feel like to have that silk tied around her wrists and ankles, she wondered? The man's cock was already at half-staff, and as he climbed on the bed and between the woman's spread legs, it jerked in response.

The man kissed the lady's plump rump, the arch of her back, her spine, all the way to her neck. The woman gave a delighted shriek as her lover's tongue curled around the shell of her ear. Heat rushed through Lillith's body, settling low into her groin. She shifted on her feet and licked her lips, waiting in anticipation.

Long, tapered fingers slid down the woman's back, over her buttocks and inner thighs, before making a slow path upward, stopping at her entrance. He slid a finger inside her, and then another, and another still. Desire coiled in Lillith's belly, the blood in her veins turning hotter by the second.

The woman arched her back as much as possible, her fingers digging into the silk beneath her as the man pumped his fingers in her using a steady rhythm. Lillith shifted on her feet as the man urged her to lift her bottom up even higher. She was dripping wet from where he'd used his fingers to pleasure her, and now he licked her slit, his tongue teasing her clit.

His hands held her hips in place and she was crying out in ecstasy as orgasm claimed her.

Janet paused long enough to take a drink of wine, but Lillith did not look away. Her body was taut with desire as the man knelt between the woman's legs and positioned his cock at her back entrance.

Certainly he was not going to sodomize her, was he?

He lubricated his cock with a bottle of oil setting on the side table, his long fingers sliding over his thick staff, before he slowly guided his cock into her back passage.

Her hands gripped the bonds tight as he sank fully into her, a heated moan leaving her lips as he began to thrust inside her, his strokes long and steady.

He stopped for an instant, playing with her nipples, toying with them, pinching, pulling them into tight nubs. Lillith's nipples pebbled against her bodice and she ached to have the same done to her.

The woman bit the pillow beneath her as the man started moving again, his strokes harder, and her buttocks jiggled with each hard thrust. The woman cried out loudly, her mouth open wide as she met her climax. The man followed behind, his buttocks clenching tight as he pumped against her, his head falling back on his shoulders, a satisfied moan on his lips.

When the man looked up at the wall where Lillith was standing, she stepped back as if she'd been burned.

Janet put the painting back in place and sat down on one of the two chairs in the small room. The entire place had been set up with one thing in mind: sex. She had never dreamed such a place existed, and now she had seen it with her own eyes.

"If I didn't know better, I'd think he was making love to his audience," Janet said in a sultry voice. "He kept looking toward the wall the whole time. Did you notice that?"

Lillith hadn't noticed, but then again, she hadn't been looking at his face.

"Quite extraordinary," she said, feeling strangely breathless.

"Indeed," Lillith replied, ready to leave the room and the

hideout altogether. She felt in need of a cup of tea, a hot bath, and the familiarity of her home.

Coming here had been a mistake, and now all she could think about was the one man she was trying to forget.

She wondered if Victor had frequented such places, and knew with a sinking feeling he surely had. Perhaps all men were the same when it came to sex: They wanted a lot, and they wanted variety. One woman was as good as the next as far as they were concerned.

"Quit feeling guilty, Lily. You are a single woman with no husband and no love interest. You have every right to explore your sexual freedom."

Not realizing her disappointment in herself was so easy to read, Lillith forced a halfhearted smile. If only she could have the same mindset as her strong-willed friend. "You are right. I know that, Janet. I just don't think this is the place for me. I don't like how it makes me feel."

"You might be surprised how in time that will change."

Lillith ran a hand over her sweaty brow. The room itself wasn't necessarily warm, but she felt extremely heated. "Have you seen that man here before? The highwayman."

Janet shook her head. "No, but then again I do not come as often as I used to. Plus, everyone uses such an array of disguises, it would be difficult to identify someone for certain."

Thank God for that.

"Have you ever been with a man in that room," Lillith said, knowing she was asking a question she had no right to, but she was curious. What made a person want to make love in front of an audience?

"Oh my goodness, no. I have no desire to show my body off to anyone but the man or woman I'm making love to."

Lillith's heart missed a beat. "Woman? You have made love to a woman?"

"That surprises you?" Janet's lips quirked. "Oh my dearest, Lily, you are even more innocent than I feared. I could teach you a thing or two."

"I admit that I am surprised. I just thought you . . . preferred men."

"I *do* prefer men, but one night a couple asked me to join them, and having had a good deal to drink, I agreed. Truth be told, it was not as odd as one would think. The woman's body was soft and supple, and I found myself forgetting that she was a woman. I was making love to someone and they were making love to me. I got completely caught up in the moment, and I have absolutely no regrets."

Lillith certainly understood about being caught up in the moment. She had done likewise with Victor, so she could understand her friend doing the same, although Lillith honestly couldn't see joining a couple in the bedchamber. She was not the kind to share a lover—because she had done so her entire marriage—nor could she make love with a complete stranger.

The doorknob rattled and Janet glanced at the door. "I suppose we should leave and let someone else be entertained."

Nodding, Lillith walked toward the door, opened it, and gasped when the highwayman stood in the doorway, blocking her way. He had his frock coat tossed over his shoulder and held on to it by a finger.

She recalled where that finger had been, where that mouth had been, and flushed to the roots of her hair. She opened her mouth to say something and then remembered the house rule not to speak to others.

The sides of his mouth lifted in a slow, easy smile, and to her horror, something tugged at her memory. There was something strangely familiar about him. Her stomach clenched tight because she knew for certain she had met this man before, and quite recently too. She just couldn't place when or where.

Janet took the initiative and squeezed in between Lillith and the man. She gave him a curt nod and pushed past him into the hallway, pulling Lillith along with her. It could have been her imagination, but she could swear she heard his laughter following her all the way down the hallway.

By the time they arrived back in the main parlor, the room was packed with new arrivals dressed in festive costumes. The air was stifling, and if it wasn't hot enough already, now it became nearly intolerable.

A tall, dark-haired man stood with a group of three friends and was dressed like a priest. His hair was drawn back into a low queue, and though the mask hid his upper face, she could still see the sharp cheekbones and chiseled jaw. His lips were beautiful, the lower much fuller than the top.

His shoulders were hidden beneath a thick black robe, but she could tell they were broad . . . like Victor's. Her stomach clenched tight. Oh dear God, what if it was Victor? The man's hair was the same color, and it did not appear to be a wig; the consistency too shiny and real looking.

Lillith's attention was diverted from the priest when the highwayman slid back into the room, as did Cleopatra, a satisfied, saucy smile on her lips as she sauntered over to Caesar, who gave her a passionate kiss.

How could they be so nonchalant about it all? What if she was the man's wife? Would he now wander off to make love with another woman and then they would be even?

The highwayman mingled with others, and Lillith wondered if he was going to actually find another lover for the night?

Perhaps she *was* a prude, like Winfred had said. No doubt her husband had attended similar parties during his lifetime. After all, he had seemed to enjoy all the vices of the rich and powerful.

Janet leaned over and whispered into her ear, "Do you wish to go?"

Relieved, Lillith nodded and headed for the hallway, never so ready to leave a place. She was in such a hurry she rushed straight into a wide chest. Strong hands reached out and steadied her, and brilliant blue eyes twinkled behind the mask. Her pulse skittered when the man's eyes narrowed in recognition.

Dear God, not again. The night was going from bad to worse, and she was lucky if she could leave with her identity safe and her reputation intact.

"Excuse me," she said, then bit her lip. Janet's eyes widened in alarm. Bloody hell, what on earth was she thinking? Why had she opened her mouth and said anything at all?

The man leaned forward, his lips touching her ear. "Why, Lily, I'm surprised to see you here."

Her heart missed a beat. Rory Rayborne. No wonder she had recognized his handsome features.

She opened her mouth, ready to deny her identity, but thought better of it. She had been found out, and now she would have to suffer the consequences.

8

Victor took the cigar smoke deep into his lungs and released it on an exhale.

He'd arrived in London late last night to find his brother out on the town and the house silent, save for the few servants milling about.

Exhausted from a recent stretch of insomnia, he'd drunk four glasses of whiskey and fallen into a fitful slumber, only to wake to the sound of Rory stumbling through the front door at six this morning.

It was now nearing four o'clock in the afternoon and Victor was losing patience with his brother, who was still abed.

Rory had invited him to a dinner party, one which a certain lady would be attending, which was why Victor had rushed to London from Rochester.

He had to see Lillith again. He missed her with a ferocity that shocked him. It was her face he saw when he opened his eyes in the morning, and his last thought was of her when he closed them at night.

The host and hostess were the Daytons, whose eldest son

had shared a room with Rory at Cambridge. Victor had met the man on several occasions but did not know him well enough to show up at his parents' home without his brother. Plus, Rory had been the one invited, along with a guest of his choosing, so he truly had Victor at his mercy.

Pacing the floor, he glanced at the clock again. Rory would sleep all night if he allowed him to. Putting his cigar out in the crystal ashtray the servant had cleaned mere minutes before, Victor walked out of the study and up the two flights of steps to Rory's bedchamber.

He knocked lightly on the door, and when he received no reply, he opened it. The heavy drapes were pulled tight, allowing almost no light into the room. Victor muttered a curse as he tripped over clothing that had been thrown haphazardly on the floor. Ripping the drapes open, he turned to the bed where Rory lay, long limbs spread in all directions, sheets wrapped about his waist.

"Wake up, Rory, it's nearly dinnertime," Victor said, half tempted to toss the glass of water from the bedside table onto his sibling's head.

Rory opened his eyes and stared up at the ceiling as though he were trying to orient himself, before stretching, the motion sending the sheet below his waist.

Victor glanced away and grimaced. "For God's sake, man, you've slept the day away. The dinner party starts in three hours."

"And you woke me now because?" Rory asked, his voice tinged with irritation.

"Because I am anxious to arrive on time. I know how long it takes you to get ready, and I'm assuming, given your late night, that you intend to take a bath before departing."

"Of course." His lips curved into a wide smile. "You are

anxious about this evening, aren't you? Would it be because of the widow?"

Victor shrugged.

"You are either very intent on winning Grandfather's watch, or you really like this woman. It is not like you to do the pursuing."

The watch had nothing to do with it. Lillith had managed to get under his skin.

Rory got out of bed and slid his drawers on haphazardly. "Oh, and speaking of your widow—guess whom I ran into last night at the latest hideaway affair?"

The hideaway was an infamous sex club for the gentry held in a grubby estate not too far from the city. It gave the attendees the anonymity they craved, while being close enough to London that a wide variety of aristocrats could attend, himself included on very rare occasions.

At this event sexual deviousness was the order of the day. "Surely you are mistaken. Lily would never attend such an event. She has guarded her reputation too diligently to even consider it."

"I assure you it was your Lily, dressed in a red wig and a scarlet gown."

There was absolutely no way Lily would ever show her face in such an establishment. The very idea was ludicrous. "That is completely absurd. It must have been someone who resembled Lillith."

"No, I swear to you, it was she," he said, taking a large drink from the glass of water on his nightstand. Victor waited patiently as he swallowed the entire glassful and set the now empty glass back down.

He wiped his mouth with the back of his hand. "She even spoke to me, and I know her voice. I tell you, it was Lillith, and she recognized me. I saw the shock in her eyes, the embarrassment at being caught there."

"What did she say?"

"Nothing. Her friend practically dragged her out. She left immediately after our exchange."

"Whom was she with?" Victor asked, his heartbeat a roar in his ears. He could not believe it, and yet, Rory would never lie to him.

"A woman."

Victor rolled his eyes. "Could you be more vague?"

"Would you prefer she be there with a man?" he said sarcastically, scratching his head.

He did have a point.

"Do you know if she was with anyone at the party?" He cleared his throat. "Alone with anyone in particular, that is."

Rory had the decency not to smirk. In fact, he even managed to look sympathetic. "You know that discretion is the order of the day at such events. . . . However, I did run into a mutual friend who offered information that you might very well be interested in."

Someone else had recognized Lily as well? This was not good. "And pray tell who would this *mutual friend* be?"

Rory cleared his throat. "Thomas Lehman."

Victor felt like someone had socked him firmly in the gut. He had heard Thomas mention seeing Lillith in London that final night at Claymoore Hall. Had they met up already, and more importantly, were they seeing each other on a more intimate level? "And?"

"Well, Thomas alluded to the fact that Lillith had watched him with another woman."

"Watched, not participated."

"He seemed quite pleased with himself. Said he put on one

hell of show and hoped the 'scarlet lady' watching him would be inclined to join him next time."

Victor cleared his throat, a thousand different thoughts running through his mind. "You are certain Lillith will be at this dinner party tonight?"

"Without question. She is a mutual friend of the Daytons, and I believe Mr. Dayton said Lillith even paid for their youngest daughter's education."

He needed to see Lily, now more than ever. "Get ready. I do not wish to be late."

Rory grinned boyishly. "Yes, sir. I wouldn't miss this for the world."

As always at such dinners, Lillith was seated between two boring men of advancing years who made little effort to include her in on the political conversation. Men—they felt women had nothing to contribute, or that they knew very little of the world around them. Men knew everything, after all.

She smiled to herself, grateful she was no longer dependent upon a husband to survive.

"I understand you are on the committee to restore the school of arts at Folkestone, Lady Nordland," said the man to her right.

Surprised she was being addressed, she sat up straighter. "Yes, I am, my lord. Are you familiar with the school?"

His gaze shifted to her bosom and she refrained from sighing heavily. "Indeed, I am. My nephew is an artist who lives in Folkestone, and he has been looking to attend the school this fall. The fire did a good deal of damage before it was put out."

"How right you are, but we have already sold a substantial number of tickets for the upcoming auction, and I'm certain the damage will be repaired. I do hope you will be attending the event," she said, wishing he would stop staring at her chest.

"Of course."

"Is your nephew anxious to attend the school?"

"Very much so. He's quite talented, too, at least in his own mind." He snorted and glanced at the man to his right, who laughed heartily.

Lillith pressed her lips together. The poor lad. She hoped he went on to become a wealthy, popular artist.

She hid a yawn behind her gloved hand. It was going to be a very long night. After not sleeping a wink last evening, she had nearly begged off on tonight's invitation but decided to not let last night's lapse of judgment get in the way of her obligations and commitments.

She realized now what a huge mistake it had been to visit the hideaway, and regretted having gone with everything she possessed. All night she had twisted and turned, wondering what on earth Rory Rayborne would say to his brother, hoping that instead he would say nothing at all.

And what of Thomas Lehman, the infamous highwayman? She had realized who those familiar features belonged to while trying to fall asleep last night. She had sat up straight in bed when she had put the pieces together, which had been the rakish smile and the slight shift of his bottom tooth. Worse still, she had already accepted an invitation to meet him at a townhouse in St. James Square. If she sent a note saying she wished to cancel, then he would know she was trying to hide something. Should she act completely innocent when they met, or should she just own up and admit to being dragged to the hideaway by her good friend?

Either way, she dreaded their next meeting.

Perhaps she would imbibe in a glass of wine later, she thought, glancing at the footman who was refilling glasses already. Or perhaps she would have a glass of scotch when she got home. Maybe it would help her sleep.

In the meantime, the tepid tea before her would have to suffice.

She brought the cup to her lips and nearly dropped it when Rory Rayborne walked into the room, followed by his brother.

Her heart nearly leapt from her chest. Victor was even more handsome than she recalled. Dressed in a black suit with a navy waistcoat and knee-high Hessians, he looked the epitome of the English lord that he was. The hostess, the boisterous Mrs. Dayton, rushed toward the duo, giggling like a girl as she welcomed the two men.

While Victor and Rory were greeted in exuberant style, Lillith considered slipping out a side door. Perhaps no one would notice, or could she say she had fallen ill and send a note explaining as much?

Her mind made up, she slowly eased the chair back away from the table when Victor turned and looked straight at her. Her throat went dry. She swallowed hard and slid her chair back in, her heart thumping in triple time.

His lips curved into a warm smile, yet there was no warmth in his eyes. Her palms started to sweat. Perhaps he was angry about her having left Claymoore Hall without saying a word to him?

Or maybe Rory had told him exactly where she'd been last night.

Damnation.

If the tables were turned, wouldn't she feel the same? Unfortunately, the answer was a resounding yes.

Mrs. Dayton showed Rory and Victor to the head of the table to sit beside her and her daughter, the lovely Arella, the daughter who was five and ten. Though not particularly beautiful with her broad nose and thin lips, Arella had a slender body and large breasts that men already had started to notice, and she had a roving eye, which at present fell on Rory and Victor with interest. Her mother had taught her well, for she sat up straight and thrust out her chest.

Victor took a seat on one side of her, Rory on the other.

Lillith had never been the type of woman to envy a younger woman. After all, she herself had been labeled one of the most handsome debutantes of the season nearly two decades before, yet she could not ignore the twinge of jealously that rushed to the surface when Victor smiled at Arella as her mother made the introductions.

To make matters worse, not once during dinner did Victor so much as look in Lillith's direction. Her dinner companions managed to include her in on their discussion, but she had lost her patience with the conversation and with Arella and Victor's flirting, to the point she nearly left the table four times before dinner's end.

When dessert had been served, she was more than ready to leave and never look back.

She had played too many games in her marriage to do so now. Yes, she had been the one to leave Claymoore Hall without saying good-bye, and Victor had every right to be angry with her, but then again, Lillith had not expected his ex-mistress to show up out of nowhere and cling to him all night long.

"It was a pleasure speaking with you both," Lillith said to her dinner companions after an elderly couple made their departure. At least she would not be the first to leave.

"You are leaving us so early, Lady Nordland?"

"I am, but I am certain I shall see you both in the near future."

Both men looked at her chest and she wondered if she had spilled soup on her bodice without realizing it. "Good evening, gentlemen."

Thank God Mr. and Mrs. Dayton were occupied conversing

with the Rayborne brothers that they did not take notice of her departure.

The second she exited the dining room, she breathed a sigh of relief. Now if the valet would get her cloak, she would be well on her way toward home, where she would pour herself a large glass of scotch and, God willing, sleep like the dead.

She was feeling more relaxed as she approached the foyer. Just a few more steps now and she was home free.

"Where are you going, Lily?"

9

Lillith's heart jolted at the sound of Victor's voice. She clearly heard the menacing tone.

She looked at the valet longingly, and taking a deep breath, she turned. "Good evening, Lord Graston."

"Lillith," he said, giving a curt nod. His hair was slightly longer than it had been weeks before, and her thighs tightened remembering how it felt to have those silky locks sliding across her skin when he'd made love to her.

Sweet wonderful love to her.

Afraid her eyes would give away her feelings, she dropped her gaze to the diamond stud in his intricately tied cravat.

"How long have you been in London?" she asked after a minute of silence, completely ignoring his earlier question. Lord how she had missed him. She had not realized how much until now.

"Last night."

Last night? Dear God, he hadn't been at the club with his brother, had he? She swallowed hard, then met his gaze once more. "Are you staying long?"

"I do not know." He shifted on his feet, and a strand of hair fell forward.

She reached out, ready to slide it over his ear, when she caught herself. What was she doing? Her hand fell to her side, but it was too late. The sides of his mouth lifted just the slightest bit.

An elderly couple walked into the hall, and Lillith moved in order to let them pass. "Well, I really should be going."

"Why? It is early yet. Is there somewhere else you need to be?"

"I'm tired," she blurted, annoyed at the strange emotions rushing through her. Normally she was in such control, but he made her feel anything but.

"Did you have a late night?" he asked.

Her heart tripped. "Not particularly." It wasn't necessarily a lie. They had been at the club for only an hour or so, and she'd returned home immediately. "I just did not sleep very well."

He took the steps that separated them and leaned in, his lips inches from hers. "Did you enjoy yourself at the hideaway, Lady Scarlet?" he whispered, his breath hot against her face.

Lady Scarlet? Oh no. "No, I did not."

His blue eyes narrowed slightly, pinning her to the spot. "Why do I not believe you?"

"I do not know," she said, angered by his reaction. No doubt he himself had been, especially since he knew about its existence to begin with, so how dare he judge her for going. "Perhaps you don't know me well enough to make that judgment."

His shoulders straightened. "Oh, I think I know you very well, Lily." His voice was silky soft.

He consumed her, his very presence making her pulse leap and her cheeks flush. Lord help her, but she wanted him so desperately. "Just because we made love doesn't mean you know me," Lillith whispered, glancing over her shoulder to make sure no one was around. Hell, she barely knew herself anymore. What had happened to her in such a short period of time? It's like she had lost all sense of decorum, all sense of self for that matter. Perhaps she had gone temporarily insane . . .

"It was more than one night, if you recall."

Yes, how could she possibly forget the liaison against the wall of the manor? She'd made love where anyone could have come across them, and given her luck, they probably had. Who knows, perhaps at this moment her name was being whispered across ballrooms and gentlemen clubs throughout London.

He brushed his fingers over his bottom lip and her traitorous eyes followed the movements. She remembered the play of those long fingers against her body, and the touch of those soft lips against her own as he kissed a trail down her stomach, over her slick mound—licking her, tasting her, bringing her to unparalleled passion.

She swallowed hard. "I need to go home."

She took a step away from him, but he grabbed her hand, his fingers curling about her wrist. "I want to come home with you, Lily."

How fast his attitude had changed in the space of a few minutes. His words elated her, and yet terrified her all at the same time. Though she'd missed him these past weeks, she'd survived. She would always survive. To give him her heart was not wise. "I can't bring you home, Victor. I have neighbors who watch my every move."

He looked disappointed, and not just by her refusal.

"You have to learn to not live your life by other people's rules, Lily."

"You say that, and yet you just judged me," she said matter-of-factly.

His brows furrowed. "I did no such thing."

"You judge me because I attended that—that—place. Do not try and tell me that you have never been yourself."

He clenched his jaw tight. "I am not angry that you went to such an event, Lillith, but angry that I was not the one to take you."

She was reminded of the couple dressed as Cleopatra and Caesar—how passionate they had been with each other even after the woman had been taken roughly by Thomas. Would Victor want to go off and explore with other people, only to meet up later and have sex with her? The thought made her stomach churn.

"I was angry that you watched another man make love to a woman." He kept his voice low, barely a whisper. "Mad that you saw his body, mad at what could have possibly been going through your mind at that moment." He leaned in, his lips brushing her ear, his incredible scent enveloping her. "I wonder, who were you thinking of when he was fucking her, Lily?"

How dare he? She lifted her chin. "If you must know, I was thinking of you."

He laughed without mirth. "I very much doubt that, Lillith."

He used her given name, a rarity for him, which meant he was cross with her. She had said too much already and revealed too much of her feelings in the process, only to have him call her a liar. "Well, I really must be going."

He reached out and took hold of her wrist. "Please, Lily. Let me stay with you, or at the very least, come home with me. It doesn't matter to me where we go—just as long as we're together."

Mr. and Mrs. Dayton appeared behind Victor, both beaming widely. Victor dropped her hand and Lillith forced a smile she didn't feel.

"Lord Graston, we thought perhaps you had become bored with our company and left," Mr. Dayton said.

"I saw my good friend Lady Nordland leaving, and I did not want her to get away before I had the opportunity to speak with her."

The hostess frowned. "You are leaving, Lady Nordland, but Arella has not yet sung, and I know you do so love her singing." Mrs. Dayton glanced at Victor. "You really must hear her, Lord Graston. She has the voice of an angel — does she not, Lady Nordland?"

Oh, for Pete's sake, the girl was good, but not that good. Lillith had been able to read people from an early age, and although Mr. and Mrs. Dayton smiled and looked concerned that she might be leaving, the truth of the matter was they were more concerned that Victor might be leaving. They had a young daughter, after all. A daughter of marriageable age.

"I wish that I could stay to hear Arella sing, for she does have a lovely voice, but I fear I do not feel very well."

Mrs. Dayton blanched. "I hope it was not the meal."

"Not at all, Mrs. Dayton. I fear I was not feeling well before I came, and as the night progressed, it has only worsened."

Mrs. Dayton placed a hand over her ample bosom. "Perhaps a good night's sleep will do you wonders."

"I'm sure it shall. Thank you, Mrs. Dayton." Lillith nodded. "Mr. Dayton. It was a beautiful dinner party." She glanced at Victor. "It was lovely seeing you again, Lord Graston."

Victor nodded and gave a courteous smile, before looking at his host. "I shall escort Lady Nordland to her carriage and will be back momentarily."

"Excellent," Mr. Dayton replied, and Mrs. Dayton's smile could only be called triumphant.

"Good night, Lady Nordland," the two said, before rushing back to the dining room and their guests.

"Let me come home with you, Lily."

"I do not think that is wise. My staff would not be prepared to—"

Victor's jaw clenched tight. "I do not understand how one night you can visit the hideaway and watch a man make love to another woman, and yet you are worried about what your staff might think if a man wakes up in your bed."

"I do not need you to understand, Lord Graston. I am merely stating that I am not comfortable doing so."

Did she sound hypocritical?

"Then come home with me."

"I believe you are committed to staying and listening to Arella sing."

"I wish to leave with you, for I would hate for you to come upon a highwayman on your way home."

Her cheeks burned. Oh dear God, that meant Rory knew about Thomas, or had Thomas himself been the one to tell? What about the strict rules of the club itself? Was it all right if members talked about each other?

With her heart pounding in her ears, she took a step away from him. "Good night, Victor."

Victor knew he was behaving childishly. His jealousy had gotten the better of him, and now the woman he cared about more than anyone else was watching him with fury. Damn it, but he couldn't get the image of her at the club from his mind. "Lily, please don't go."

She shook her head and rushed for the door, ignoring the valet who held out a cloak.

"Let me hail your driver," the valet said, but Lillith motioned him off with a wave of her hand.

"Do not bother. I know where he is parked," Lillith said, forgetting her cloak as she pushed the front door open and rushed down the steps.

Victor took the cloak from the valet's hands and followed behind her. The air was crisp and cool, and she had to be freezing in her thin gown as she walked down the sidewalk in long strides.

"Lily!" he said, nearly running to catch up with her.

She stopped, her shoulders rigid, chin held high, the wind whipping the gown, showing her long legs and shapely behind. He could not look away. He wanted her desperately. "Come home with me, Lily."

He took her hand and slid his fingers through hers. At first she didn't respond, but then the long, elegant fingers curled around his and tightened. "My driver is just over there." She motioned for him to come over and the old servant nodded.

He helped her with her cloak, and they waited in silence as the carriage pulled up to where they stood. The driver jumped down from his perch and flipped the stairs down.

Victor helped her in. "I shall be right back," he said, returning to the party just long enough to give his well wishes and tell his brother that he would see him back at the townhouse. Rory had smiled knowingly and returned his full attention to the charming Arella.

Half expecting the carriage to have left without him, Victor breathed a sigh of relief to find Lily waiting for him. He waved the man off as he started to climb down. "Eighteen Compton Street."

"Yes, my lord."

Lillith's eyes widened when he climbed in and took the seat beside her. Did she think he would not be returning?

"I do not want you to leave the party on my account," she said, pressing her lips together.

"The only reason I attended the party to begin with was because I knew you would be here."

Her eyes narrowed. "Is that true?"

"Yes, my brother wrote me in Rochester and told me of the dinner party, and let me know that you would be in attendance. I rushed to London in order to be here."

The information pleased her—he could tell by the light in her eyes and the slight curve of her lips, even if her silence said otherwise.

"And I am glad I did."

She smiled for the first time that night and his heart skipped a beat.

"The Daytons will be horribly disappointed," she said, her voice brimming with sarcasm.

"They did not seem too disappointed, as Rory was being quite attentive."

She actually laughed a little, then glanced out the window, no doubt looking to see if anyone had noticed their departure. They were in London, so there would be talk that they had both disappeared together. She just needed to learn how to ignore the gossips. Within days it would be old news.

She glanced over at him, the smile on her lips faltering. The pulse in her throat quickened as he leaned over and kissed the delicate skin of her neck.

She released her breath on a sigh.

It seemed like he had only stepped into the carriage when it rolled to a stop. They were at the townhouse already?

Though Victor yearned to lift Lillith in his arms and race up the steps, he knew she would fight him, and it would not be wise when she worried so much about what others thought. Indeed, she was probably now concerned that someone would recognize her carriage dropping them off in front of his family's townhome. She would not think to explain that her niece was newly engaged to Sinjin. It did not matter that Sinjin was not in residence currently. Anything could be explained.

He stepped out of the carriage and extended his elbow. She slid her hand around his arm and they walked up the steps where they were met at the door by Jeffries, the family's faithful valet who had come to London with Rory.

Jeffries shut the door behind them and helped Lillith out of her cloak. "My lord, may I get you anything?"

"No, I shall be retiring for the night."

"Very well, my lord."

Victor couldn't resist—he swooped Lillith up in his arms. She gave a screech and buried her face in his neck, embarrassed. He savored the sweet smell of her, the touch of her lips against his throat.

Already his body was on fire. He yearned to take her beneath him and bring her to climax over and over again. They were no longer at Claymoore Hall, surrounded by gossiping mothers, debutantes, and chaperones. They could do what they wanted and no one would be the wiser, save for his servants, but they would never utter a word. They were paid well for a reason.

At the door to his chamber, he let Lillith down, her body sliding against his the entire way. He loved her body, her full breasts, the soft curve of her hips, and the legs that kept going. Already he could envision those long limbs wrapped about his waist.

He opened the door and motioned for her to go ahead of him. He'd had the room decorated in dark colors and warm, rich woods, and the thick velvet drapes kept the cold London air from creeping in. Ever since he was a boy, his room had always been a sanctuary, a place for him to get away from the world at large, to close the drapes and forget about everything.

Lillith's fingers brushed along a side table he had bought

while in Italy. The craftsmanship was incredible; the polish so smooth you could see your own reflection. She walked toward the fireplace mantel. As always, Jeffries kept a fire going, and the coals burned bright but didn't put off too much heat.

Victor shrugged out of his jacket and tossed it over a chair. Lillith picked up the book on his bedside table, read the spine, and then glanced at him. "You read Burns?"

"Yes, he's a favorite. Why do you sound surprised?"

She shrugged. "I know he has a popular female following. I just never thought you would be among his fans."

"He is quite the scoundrel."

"Spoken like a man who knows a thing or two about scoundrels."

He liked the playfulness in her voice, the wistfulness of her smile, the easy manner about her. When he got her alone she was such a different person from what the rest of the world saw. Behind that prim exterior was a lighthearted vixen just begging to get out.

"Your home is lovely, Victor."

"Technically, it is my parents' home, though my brothers and I spend more time here than they do."

"I noticed your father was not at Claymoore Hall during the party."

Victor's father had taken ill some weeks before, and his poor health had been the reason behind the ultimatum to marry. Victor had seen his father when he'd returned from Claymoore Hall, and his fragile appearance had been shocking. His father was tall, well over six feet, but had always carried his weight proportionately. In the past few weeks he had lost nearly two stone and it showed on his frame.

"I'm sorry, did I speak out of turn?"

"No, not at all. It's just that my father is not well."

"I am sorry, Victor," she said earnestly. "I shall pray that he grows stronger and will recover soon."

"Thank you," he said, resting his hip against the bed. How glad he was to have her here. Finally. Lord how he had missed her.

"And what of your family, Lillith? Do they live nearby?"

"I have a sister, Katelyn and Marilyn's mother, and she lives in London for the most part. Our parents died when we were quite young, and my grandmother, God rest her soul, died just last year. She was a lovely woman, and I adored her. She was so strong and witty. Honestly, she could do anything a man could do, but better."

He laughed, enjoying the smile that lit her face at talk of her beloved grandmother. "She sounds like you."

She laughed under her breath. "No, she was much stronger than I am. She was born poor. Her father was a farmer, and she would go with her mother to the village, where they would sell their goods. My grandfather, a young, adventurous baron, saw her and instantly became smitten. Each week he would come to the village and buy from her and only her. It got to the point where he would buy nearly everything she and her mother brought with them. He asked her one day if she would marry him, and she said no, because marrying him would cause her to leave her mother, and who would do the work since she was the oldest and had no brothers?"

"And what was his response?"

"He said that if she would marry him, he would buy the farm and buy the goods produced in order to keep his household running."

"Did he keep his word?"

"Indeed, he did. He made my grandmother's life, and that of her parents, easier in the process. I respect him and my grandmother immensely, especially when they took us in after my mother died. It could not have been easy to raise two girls when they had already raised their own children, but they did so, and I will forever be grateful."

"I am sure they were proud of the woman you've become."

Lillith smiled softly. "I think they were. I hope they were. I miss them both very much."

"Tell me, did your grandmother approve of your husband?"

10

The smile slid from Lillith's face and she took a deep breath. "At first, yes. Everyone approved of my marriage. Winfred was well respected amongst the aristocracy, especially for championing many lesser-known causes. When he came courting, my entire family was shocked and delighted. I honestly could not believe he would be interested in me. I was deeply honored and felt we would complement each other in many ways."

"How did he know you? Were your families connected?"

She shook her head. "No, his father knew my grandfather, but I saw him for the first time in Hyde Park when I was with my sister. My grandmother had taken us to have a picnic, and that afternoon we rode about the park in her new phaeton. Winfred was on horseback, riding with a good friend of his, and they stopped us. I thought he was interested in my sister." She played with the ring on her finger. "Most men were. Loraine is extremely outgoing and has a true gift for conversation, where I am quite shy."

Victor smiled to himself. She was reserved and quiet, but he quite liked that quality, though one would not know it from the company he had previously favored, like Selene, who craved attention from everyone.

"Anyway, Winfred soon started calling on me. We would go on rides and picnics, and were always well chaperoned. His mother insisted upon it and would oftentimes accompany us herself."

"How long did he court you for?"

She tapped a finger against her lips as she thought about his question. "I think it was on our sixth outing that he asked me to marry him. I was stunned, but excited. I had always wanted to be a wife, and many of my friends were already engaged or married, so I was ready."

"Did you live in London?"

"No, we lived in Bath, though Winfred would often spend months at a time in London at our townhouse."

"Which is where you live now?"

"Yes." She did not elaborate, and he wondered if he was asking too many questions. The change in her demeanor from the time he'd asked about her grandmother to talking about her husband had been obvious.

"I learned early on that Winfred had a passion for drink . . . and for men."

He was stunned when she continued talking about her husband, and he had no wish to stop her. In the past few days he'd inquired about the late Lord Nordland and learned that the man's sexuality was no secret from the *ton,* his exploits talked about all over London. He'd been known to frequent clubs with young men on either arm, and he liked them young, very slight and frail. It wasn't his sexuality that bothered Victor most, since he had a few friends who preferred the same sex and they were good people, but it was the way Winfred had treated Lillith that had been unforgivable. His cruelty was renowned, and he was stunned that she had withstood it all and come out unscathed.

How shocking it must have been for a young girl who had

been courted so gallantly by a wealthy and titled man to learn that she was marrying a two-faced philanderer.

"I suppose I am thankful for Winfred in one regard."

"Which would be?"

"He taught me to always look beyond the exterior, for one can hide a lot behind a smile and a kind word. I have gotten to the point where I can read people quite well."

"And what do you see when you look at me?" he asked, brushing a hand through his hair, almost sorry that he'd asked the question.

She squared her shoulders. "I see an extremely handsome young man standing before me. The fine material of his coat and the exquisite tailoring tells me he is made of money, not to mention the glittering diamond at his throat."

Victor winced. He had worn the diamond only as an afterthought. He felt guilty that he had done so to impress others. He'd had a feeling he would be the man with the highest title at the dinner, and he'd wanted Lillith to know it. "What else?"

"The way he holds himself tells me he has grace, and his charm says he knows his power over people, especially women."

Her critique made him nervous, which surprised him. He normally never cared what anyone thought of him. "You know what you want and you are accustomed to getting it."

Now she was making him sound like a selfish boy, and yet she was not too far off the mark.

She dropped her gaze and smiled. "And now that I have described you, what do you have to say about me?"

He stood and took the few steps that separated them. She lifted her gaze to meet his, and he noticed the pulse fluttering at her throat. Her beautiful hazel eyes danced, and yet he saw a certain vulnerability there that made his heart clench. She had been so very wounded in her time.

"I see a beautiful, mature woman."

Her brows furrowed. "Mature? Why do you not just say old." She said the words teasingly, and he smiled, relieved to see her good humor had returned in force.

"Old? Oh no, you are not old. You are a woman of the world. A woman who knows what she wants," he said, throwing her own words back at her. "But you're oftentimes afraid to go after what you desire. You're too afraid of what everyone thinks . . . because you have spent a lifetime shielding yourself from gossip. You have built an image of yourself—a good woman, a virtuous woman, who many aspire to be like. What if they knew the truth; that you yearn to throw caution to the wind, to taste, feel, and experience everything that life has to offer? Have you wondered what it would feel like not to be afraid of who you truly are, and not what you have made yourself be?"

Her throat convulsed as she swallowed hard, but she held his gaze. "I have worked hard for my reputation out of necessity. You have no idea what it is like to walk down the street and have other women whispering behind their fans about you and your dreadful marriage, or to have men smirking at you, knowing full well what is happening, or not happening, behind the closed doors of your own home."

"No, I do not know what that kind of abuse feels like, Lily. I imagine it could not have felt good."

"Have you ever heard a terrible rumor about yourself?"

"Once, when I attended a country party in the Lake District it was reported that I spent the night with four different ladies in the course of one evening."

Lillith rolled her eyes. "Four in one evening? Could a man possibly have that much stamina?"

He shrugged, trying with difficulty to keep the smile off his face.

"You did not," she said, adding a gasp for good measure.

"I did."

She shook her head, then bit her bottom lip. "If I wondered about the label of rakehell before, now I understand how well deserved said label is."

"There are rakes who deserve the title more than I."

"Do you actually mean to tell me you do not feel you deserve to be labeled a rakehell?" She did not keep the humor from her voice.

"I have had a lot of lovers, and I've not once apologized for that. I would much rather have someone say that I have lived my life by my rules rather than by someone else's."

Which reminded Lillith of how very different she and Victor were. Where he had lived by his own rules, she had, in turn, lived by society's rules, which was quite sad when she thought about it. What would it feel like to live life on your own terms, she wondered? Actually, she had done just that by going to the hideaway. She was taking a chance, and in some ways it felt liberating, and other ways it felt wrong.

"Men think you are a beautiful woman who has been treated badly and come out the other side of a horrible relationship wiser and even more amazing than when you went in. Quit living your life for the masses and live it for yourself, Lily. I want to show you another life. One that is exciting. One that you deserve. Will you let me show you how good it could be?"

He sensed her excitement, but also her trepidation. "What does that life entail?"

"Anything you desire . . ." Victor said, untying his cravat, all the while not taking his eyes off Lillith.

She felt positively breathless, her heart pounding against her breastbone.

"I've missed you, Lily," he said, his voice like the smoothest whiskey. "I've dreamt of you, I've longed for you."

Her knees felt as weak as her resolve.

His gaze shifted over her, making her feel like she had not a single stitch of clothing on. He was like a drug to her senses, and she knew she would never get enough of him . . . ever. What would it be like to have him in her life every single day?

She did not pretend that she was even in the running to be his wife, but she was flattered by his attention and wondered, like most young women, what it would feel like to have him as a husband. She would be the envy of all her friends, and probably every young debutante too.

Why had he followed her to London? He had already had her. She would have thought he'd be done with her and that would be it.

But he had come after her. He knew where she had been last night, knew what she had done, and he had been mad, jealous even, and still he wanted her.

He reached for her, his hands cupping her face, his thumbs sweeping along her jaw. The way he looked at her made her feel like the most desirable woman in the world. She hoped she never forgot this feeling or the sensations coursing through her, or the intense need and passion she felt whenever she looked into his long-lashed, brilliant blue eyes.

She leaned into him, surprised at how fast his heart was racing. Her feet left the ground and he was walking them toward the bed, then depositing her onto the thick blankets.

He followed her onto the mattress, his arms on either side of her as he looked down at her, his long hair brushing her shoulder. He bent his head, then kissed her neck and the slope of each breast. She felt a tug, and her breasts were bared above the bodice of her gown.

His large hand covered a globe, the nipples stabbing into his palm as he bent his head to kiss the other breast, his tongue swirling around the rigid peak. Lillith's breath left her in a rush at the delicious sensations, at the way he used a combination of licking, pinching, and sucking to make her body sing.

Cool air hit her legs, and the next thing she knew her skirts were shoved up above her waist and he was using his knees to spread her thighs wide. She always felt so feminine when she was with him, and she savored the sensation of being taken.

Her need was so great, she didn't want to wait another second to have him inside her.

"Victor," she whispered, and he opened his eyes. He must have seen the need in her face and heard the plea in her voice, because he unbuttoned his trousers and slid his hard length into her in one quick motion.

Her breath left her in a rush as he filled her completely, his large cock stretching her.

Victor released a contented sigh as Lillith's creamy inner walls gripped him tight. He buried his face in her neck, inhaling deeply of her scent as he kissed the racing pulse at her throat.

She spread her thighs wider, cupping her hips, taking him deeper inside her body. Her hands moved to his back, pressing against the strong muscles there, her nails skimming his shoulders.

He made love to her with a tenderness that shocked her. He made her feel cherished, his blue eyes intense as he stared down at her.

He shifted ever so slightly, putting just the right pressure on her clit. Each thrust was harder, more purposeful, and she let out a heated moan when he took her nipple into his mouth and sucked.

Her head fell back on the mattress, her mouth open as the multiple sensations washed over her, bringing her to a shattering climax that had her calling out his name.

He kept stroking slowly as the throbbing subsided. Then he went up on his knees and eased her hips up, and her legs wide and high. He started with shallow thrusts, and at this angle she could feel every hard inch of him as he teased the sensitive patch of skin within her pulsing inner walls.

The thick crown of his cock slid out of her, and he stayed there, teasing her folds. She looked up at him, her hips lifting. She needed him inside her. "Victor," she said, her voice thick with desperation.

She looked down between their bodies, at the huge cock positioned at her slick entrance. He eased into her and she sighed with relief, her hand moving to his ballocks where she stroked the delicate patch of skin that Janet had told her made men crazy.

Victor released a low, ragged moan as he lifted her legs over his shoulders and thrust against her. Her hands squeezed his buttocks tightly, the muscles clenching beneath her fingers.

The now-familiar stirrings of climax began again, and as he ground against her, asserting just the right pressure against her clit, she came again. His moan mingled with hers, and together they reached for the stars.

Victor pulled her into his arms and kissed her forehead. "Will you stay?"

It was horribly late, and she hated the thought of venturing out into the cold night. Leaving the warm sanctuary of his arms for the coldness of her bed was not at all appealing.

"I will, but I should leave early before anyone sees me."

To his credit, he didn't say anything about their discussion earlier—how she should stop worrying about what others thought of her. "Then perhaps you should stay until the afternoon or evening?"

She frowned and he laughed; the sound was like music to her ears. "Are you challenging me to see if I will really stay?"

A smile teased his lips. "Perhaps."

11

Marilyn watched her mother and her much y
thony beneath lowered lashes. Since arrivin
raine had pretended to be the doting mother
been. She had arrived on Aunt Lillith's doors
planation of how things had gone so horribl
moore Hall and demanded they stay with h
died down.

On the contrary, everything had turned o
Katelyn, and now she was marrying a man s
adored.

But Loraine would never see it that way.
ried that Lord Balliford's family, if he had an
ing with their hand out, seeking the money
paid for Katelyn's hand.

The fact of the matter was there was no m
Loraine had no doubt spent every last schil
townhouse and her lover, who had all the t
man from his shiny new clothes to his air of
Oh well, Marilyn could fake it with the

ounger lover An-
; in London, Lo-
hat she never had
ep wanting an ex-
y wrong at Clay-
r until the gossip

ıt for the best for
.e truly loved and

She was too wor-
, would be arriv-
Loraine had been

ney to be had, for
ng on the rented
appings of a kept
onfidence.
est of them, too,

n to a man three
ghter.
l her way when
uncomfortable,
England for her

ıt ball for you, I
tion in the long
ith, Loraine did
ear, she did not

re a gown that
ast ten years her

.oraine said, her

ee, smirked, and
r. "Yes, we are
thens, near An-
ıan welcome to
no such thing.
summer here in

nilar in shape to
e so much for so
t that always the
he truly humble
ometimes.
y interested in?"
cheeks. It was a
she was getting
get her mother

started, because once she said a man's name, Loraine would be relentless in her pursuit to see her married off. Then her responsibilities toward her daughters would be well and truly over. Did she forget that she had a thirteen-year-old son, Marilyn wondered, thinking of her poor brother who languished in a boarding school in the north of England. Like Marilyn, he was probably a bastard, too.

"Perhaps you can follow in Katelyn's footsteps and marry one of the Rayborne brothers?"

How convenient that would be. "I have already told you that I consider Rory and Victor my friends, Mother, but they will never be anything more."

Loraine frowned. "A pity. It could have made matters so much easier."

The overworked maid walked into the parlor without knocking and gave a halfhearted curtsy. "Madam, there is a young lady here who has asked for Lady Marilyn."

Loraine's brows rose. "And did you manage to get a name?" she asked, rolling her eyes in exasperation.

The maid managed to school her features. From the moment Marilyn and Katelyn had entered their mother's house, it had been obvious the girl could not stand Loraine and vice versa. "Yes, she says her name is Lady Anna."

Marilyn's pulse skittered. She had met Lady Anna at Claymoore Hall, and they had started a strange relationship of sorts when Anna had begun flirting with her. Indeed, they had even kissed, and Marilyn had left the room weak-kneed and trembling. She still did not understand the depth of her feelings for the young noblewoman, but she had hoped time away would clear her mind.

But Anna had come calling, and Marilyn must face her feelings head-on.

"Shall I have her come in?" the maid asked.

Marilyn nodded. "Of course."

"Who is Lady Anna?" Loraine asked glancing at Anthony, who sat up and straightened his jacket, no doubt ready to impress.

"A friend I met at Claymoore Hall."

Loraine released a breath. "Well, I shall let the two of you catch up. Come, Anthony, let us give Marilyn time alone with her friend."

Marilyn could hear her heart race as her mother left the room with Anthony in tow. She had not seen Anna since Claymoore Hall, and that had been an odd encounter, one that she had not been able to purge from her thoughts since.

The maid entered a moment later, followed by Anna. She looked beautiful in a cream-colored walking gown embroidered with petite roses. She had a bloom in her cheeks, and her dark eyes sparkled as they fell on Marilyn.

"Can I get you tea?" the maid asked.

"Yes, thank you."

"Actually, I cannot stay long."

"A pity," Marilyn said, actually relieved.

Anna waited until the maid left before she closed the steps that separated them and smiled. "I have missed you, my dear friend. Tell me, have you thought of me these past weeks?"

What game did she play at? Rumors of her sordid behavior at Claymoore Hall had reached London. Marilyn was stunned she had not stayed in the York countryside with her grandparents to weather the storm. But apparently she did not care what others thought.

Marilyn swallowed past the sudden lump in her throat. If she had learned anything from her aunt, it was not to show too much of yourself to the outside world. She did not wish to be vulnerable in any way, especially since she remembered well what Victor had said about Anna and her sexual nature. She knew how to play the game and play it well.

"I have thought of you. You are my friend, after all," Marilyn managed after a few awkward moments.

Anna tilted her head to the side. "Is that all we are, Marilyn? Just friends?"

Marilyn shifted on her feet, feeling at a true disadvantage. "I believe so."

Anna reached up, took a lock of Marilyn's hair, and wound it around a finger. She brought it to her nose and inhaled deeply, her lips curving into a sweet smile. "You are truly beautiful, Marilyn. Your eyes are in such contrast to your hair." She released the curl, the backs of her fingers brushing over Marilyn's nipple.

Strange emotions rushed through Marilyn, and she fought the sudden urge to run away, far from the desire raging within her.

Anna spied Marilyn's body's reaction, for her gaze focused on her breasts for a moment, before drifting lower and back up again.

Marilyn remembered the fiery kiss they had shared, the exquisite heat that they had generated.

She cleared her throat. "Why are you here, Anna?"

"Is that not obvious, Marilyn?" she asked in a silky-soft voice.

Marilyn licked lips that had suddenly gone dry, and before she could form a reply, Anna leaned in and kissed her, her lips soft and supple. She tasted like sweets, smelled like ambrosia, and Marilyn was lost to all thought.

Lady Anna's arms wrapped around her waist, pulling her tight, and Marilyn could feel her heart pounding against her breastbone in time with Anna's. For all her cool composure, she too was feeling the effects of the kiss.

She deepened the kiss, and her hands were moving down Marilyn's body, cupping her bottom, pulling her close.

The world could have caught fire and Marilyn would not have been aware of it, too in the moment and the feelings rushing through her.

Lord help her, but she wanted more, craved more, and it scared her, especially when there was so much expectation for her to marry soon.

Could she marry and take a lover, she wondered? Perhaps a female lover, or did she find Anna interesting and exciting because she was so different from anyone she'd met? She had not felt this way about anyone else, male or female.

Anna's hand slipped beneath Marilyn's skirts, up over her drawers, to the slit. Her instinct was to push away, and yet when Anna's fingers slid over her heated flesh, the breath left her lungs.

"So sweet," Anna whispered against her lips, her fingers parting her as she touched the small bundle of nerves at the top of her sex.

Anna slid a finger inside and Marilyn forgot to breathe.

The door opened and a loud gasp filled the air.

Marilyn jumped away, but it was too late. Her mother and sister stood before her, mouths dropped open, disbelief in both their eyes. Loraine looked from Marilyn to Anna and back again.

Marilyn had the sense to smooth out her skirts.

"What are you doing, Marilyn?" Loraine asked, her voice holding a slight edge as she took a step toward them.

Katelyn reached out and grabbed her arm. "Mother, please."

Marilyn tried to think of any excuse that would explain her kissing the other woman, and yet, she knew her mother would never believe it, so she stayed silent.

Anna's gaze skipped from Loraine to Katelyn. "It's lovely to see you again, Lady Katelyn."

"I would kindly ask you to leave, Lady Anna" Loraine said.

"Moth
would no
She op
thrown ou
"Moth
lyn said, a
Marily
her about
eyes.
"I wou
Loraine sa
find husba
Anna fl
her feature
A mom
plain herse
"I cann
ing her he
isted withi
"Mothe
uncalled fo
"I woul
to find yo
trembling
sympatheti
Marilyn
"Aunt
softly Mari
and clear.
mouth, so l
Katelyn
her mother
"Stop it

going to marry very
what you saw."
Loraine stared at
ment. "I am glad to
She walked for the
back.
Katelyn brushed
"Marilyn, I am sorry
from walking in. She
said I should join yo
"It is not your fau
"But I should hav
"Do you judge m
Her brows furro
are my sister and I s
Tears burned her
Katelyn hugged
marriage. I know th
"Yes, I know you
Putting her at ar
Anna?"
"I do not know.
that much."
"Just guard your
Those were not
since Victor had w
woman's reputation
"I will. I am sure

Lillith's skin, soothing
e sun filtered in through
elf, content and happier
oon, and she and Victor
fast fit for a king and
en set up in the sitting
the garment falling just
eyes had turned a shade
made it through break-
had no more sat back in
he table and then taken
thless.
?" he asked, his breath
d?" She said the words
t meant them. Surely he

would grow weary of having her here, he, a man used to having his own space. Plus, he shared the home with his brothers. Thank goodness Sinjin was still in Rochester, but Rory would come home soon and she dreaded that moment. Hopefully he never mentioned the hideaway or the Scarlet Lady.

Victor's hands covered both breasts as he teased her nipples into tight buds. It was like an invisible thread was being pulled taut between her breasts and her sex.

As he continued to tease her, she felt his cock grow hard, pressing into her back like hot steel.

Her inner muscles tightened, pulsing with need.

She looked back at him, saw the heat in his eyes as he slid a hand from her breasts to her belly, to slide between her legs, his fingers teasing her clit.

A long finger slid inside her, joined by another. As he pumped his hand against her, the water spilled over the side of the tub and onto the floor.

"The water," she said, her hips lifting to meet his hand.

"Then we shall get out before Jeffries comes to tell me the ceiling is caving in," he said with a smile, urging her to stand.

She could feel his gaze on her, was mindful that it was daytime, and that despite the fact that the drapes were drawn, he could still see every flaw.

Glancing back at him, her heart missed a beat. He was perfection, his muscles defined by the water and oil that slid off his body. Even his cock was magnificent, standing proudly from a nest of dark hair.

He helped her dry off, lingering on her bottom and breasts. She didn't make it two steps when he bent her over the arm of a chair, his cock probing her sex. He slid into her easily, and she was shocked at how full she was in this position, how positively stuffed she felt, like she couldn't take another inch.

He moaned and slowly began to move, his thrusts long and

steady as he gripped tight to her hips. "Touch yourself," he said, and her breath caught in her throat. She had touched herself on several occasions and had always felt odd and guilty doing so.

But at Victor's request, she touched her breast. His hand covered hers a second later. "Do you like your nipples to be lightly touched, or do you like more pressure? Do you want them pinched or pulled?" As he asked, he did just that, and to her shock, she realized she liked this little experiment.

"I like it harder."

He grinned, white teeth flashing in his tan face.

His other hand moved to her sex, his fingers toying with her tiny button, sliding over it, around it, over and over again, all the while he played with her breasts, giving attention to one, then the other. "Touch yourself here."

She did exactly what he told her to do, her fingers sliding over her soft folds. She was hot and wet, making it easy for her fingers to glide over her clit.

His hot breath fanned against the back of her neck; then his lips were there, kissing a path down her spine as he eased a finger inside her back passage. Her breath caught in her throat at the odd sensation that was a combination of pleasure and pain.

To be filled by his cock and his finger with just the slightest sliver of skin between was amazing, and she felt her body climb closer to orgasm with each thrust.

Her fingers pressed harder against her tiny button, while with her free hand she clung to the back of the chair, which moved along the floor with each steady stroke.

"That's it, Lily. Reach for it."

She came with a satisfied moan, her fingers easing up as her quim pulsed and throbbed.

Victor's thrusts grew more shallow and fast, and with a deep-throated groan, he came, filling her with his thick cream.

* * *

Selene stared back at her reflection. Her brown eyes looked dead in her pale face, her painted red lips spread in a thin line. She was just twenty-five, and yet she felt twice that. She had made a lot of mistakes in her life, but none so great as playing Victor Rayborne for a fool.

Victor had been a generous lover, and she had been smitten from the moment he had walked into her tiny dressing room on the back side of the small theater. She had only a bit part as a milkmaid, and yet many a man had taken notice of her, but Victor had stood out from amongst all her suitors in both looks and wealth.

And he had bought her pretty trinkets and taken her out on the town, treating her like a princess. He didn't mind the way people watched them, or how the aristocracy looked down their noses at her.

With his blessing, she had continued her acting career, and he never seemed to mind the whistles from other men when she came on the stage. Why had that not been enough for her? Why had she allowed herself to reach for more? Victor had been the second son of a very wealthy and highly respected earl, but a second son had not been good enough for her.

No, she had wanted to be the mistress of the most powerful man in London. Well, she had gained a count now, a man with money to burn, and yet she had never been so miserable in all her life. And Howard was half the man Victor was—in both stature and in terms of below the belt. But she had figured a few minutes on her back each night was little to put up with when she had a fashionable flat in the West End, jewelry to rival any duchess, and more servants than she required, all of whom answered to her every whim.

And she would trade every last thing her count had given her for Victor Rayborne. She wanted him back, and she would do anything in her power to possess him.

She had thought she could walk into Claymoore Hall and he would be elated to see her, overjoyed even. But that had not at all been the case. He had been shocked to see her, and not in a good way. She had seen the look of disdain in his eyes. He'd wanted her gone, and it had cut to the quick.

"There you are, my dear."

Selene had actually hoped Howard wouldn't show tonight.

"I'm on in five minutes, Howard. Perhaps you should find your seat."

He frowned and continued unbuttoning his trousers. "Not so fast, my dear."

"Howard, I will be late."

"Nonsense. It won't take but a moment."

She bit her lip to keep from sighing with agitation and got into position, turning her back to him, her hands braced on the vanity, her legs spread wide apart, just as he liked.

He reached for the slit in her drawers, running his hands roughly over her flesh.

"You're dry, my dear," he said, sliding a finger into his mouth before inserting it inside her.

She forced a response.

"You're on in five minutes, Selene. Are you ready?" Francesca, her manager, called from the door.

"Yes, I'll be right there." She'd barely gotten the words out when Howard stuck his small prick inside her.

He watched her in the mirror, his gaze fastened on her breasts that bounced with each hard thrust. He was already out of breath.

She was relieved when he reached for the kerchief in his jacket pocket and pulled out of her seconds later, spilling his seed into the cloth, jerking as he groaned like a pig.

He already had seven children with his wife, and he was always extremely careful with her.

There would be no divorce. She would forever be the other woman with her count.

"I'll go take my place," he said, giving her a quick kiss as he shoved his cock back into his trousers.

She pushed her skirts down and nodded. "I shall see you after."

He lifted her chin with firm fingers. "I will have eyes only for you, my love."

She nodded. "I know, Howard. I know."

The door closed behind him, then opened seconds later. Selene looked up at her manager and sighed. The woman's auburn wig was ridiculous, nearly swallowing her large face with its bulbous nose and small, beady eyes. "You ready, my dear?"

"Of course." She forced a smile she didn't feel. Howard had started to rule her life. She had gone from performing four days a week, to only one, by Howard's insistence. And every week he positioned himself in the front row, center stage, as though to say "I own her." Worse still, before she went on, he made sure to visit her in her dressing room and fuck her, just as he had tonight. Always it was the same; he waited until she was dressed and in full makeup, and minutes from going onstage. A part of her wondered if he was making love to the character, but after a while she didn't care.

"What's wrong, my darling?"

Tears welled in her eyes. "I miss him."

"Who do you miss? Your count? He only just left . . ."

"Good God, no! I miss Victor."

Francesca's lips curved into a smile. "Ah, the beautiful one."

Yes, the beautiful one. And he was lovely, in every way. What a fool she had been to think he would want her back. She shook her head, furious at herself for reaching too high. She had told no one about her trip to Claymoore Hall. In truth, she didn't want to risk Howard finding out. Instead, she had told him she was heading to York to see her ailing aunt. Upon her return, Howard had asked a thousand questions, making her wonder if perhaps he'd had her followed.

After an enthusiastic sexual greeting on her part, he had simmered down, but the leash was growing ever so tight. He must know of her true feelings, else he would not be acting so . . . desperate. The question was, if she broke it off with Howard, would it matter and would Victor want her? It was a huge risk to take, especially now that she knew he liked the widow Nordland.

Francesca patted her hand. "You will get him back, my darling. You are the most beautiful woman in London, and no man can resist you."

A few weeks ago she would have believed her, but she had seen the way Victor stared at Lillith, who was a lady in every sense of the word.

A lady was something that she would never be. After all, money couldn't buy blue blood.

Her mind returned to that night at Claymoore Hall when she had gone looking for Victor in the gardens. He had met her on the pathway and appeared to be winded.

Only one activity would cause Victor to be winded. Her gaze had scanned the vicinity, and if she had not known better, she would say by the way he'd blocked her path that he was hiding a lover's identity. Although hurt and distraught by the thought he had just been having a liaison, she played nice and tried everything in her power to get him to come to her room.

But he'd declined. There had been absolutely no interest on his part.

Selene glanced at her reflection, lifted her chin, and took a deep, steadying breath. "I hope you are right, Francesca," she said, determined that no matter what it took, Victor Rayborne would be hers once more.

13

Loraine walked around the townhouse parlor, her gaze skipping over every little detail.

Lillith's nails dug into the arm of the chair. Her sister didn't miss a thing, her gaze lingering on the flowers Victor had sent over this morning. The roses of varying shades in an emerald vase sat on a side table. Thank goodness Lillith had slid the card into her desk, far away from prying eyes. Just like she knew she would, Loraine searched the bouquet and the vicinity for any sign of whom they were from.

"You have an admirer, I see."

Lillith cleared her throat. "They are from a friend."

Loraine's brows lifted and a small smile touched her lips. "Speaking of admirers—I wanted to address this little coming-out party that you have arranged for my daughter."

"I have no desire to step on your toes, Loraine. I thought you were leaving town and I did—"

Loraine clucked her tongue, something their grandmother had done for the slightest misdeed, an irritating gesture that had always driven Lillith crazy. "Do not be silly. I spoke to Marilyn excited about the ball. If I were

p," Lillith said, knowing no such
ys been intensely self-serving. She
foremost.

nnection with one of Sinjin's broth-
elieve, and I was hoping that perhaps
that direction."

ped. "They seem to have developed a
friendship."

"Well, many a marriage started off in friendship, only to grow to love," Loraine said matter-of-factly.

Actually, Lillith knew of very few arranged marriages that had ended happily. Normally the couple spent time in separate homes, as far away from each other as possible.

"Perhaps you can convince Marilyn to consider Victor."

Lillith could not possibly imagine how horrifying it would be to have Marilyn marry Victor. "You do know that Lord Balliford knew the truth of Marilyn's parentage and used that information in order to force Katelyn to marry him?"

Loraine flinched as though Lillith had struck her. "Yes, I read it in your very detailed letter, but surely the secret has died with him."

"Sinjin knows the truth, Loraine. I have to believe he would share that information with his family, given how he would want them to know the details in case they were ever approached."

She lifted her chin a few inches. "Are you saying my daughter is not good enough for a second son?"

"You know that is not at all what I am saying. I believe any man would be fortunate to have Marilyn as a wife. I just think it would be best to have Marilyn choose her own mate; no matter who that might be. She can reach as high as she wants to—she is a beautiful young woman and very well liked."

"Yes, well, looks will only get you so far. I just do not want her putting any man off because she is not in love." She snorted as though the idea of marrying for love was silly.

Edward appeared in the doorway of the parlor and cleared his throat.

It was not like her valet to be so secretive. She stood and walked over to him. "Lord Graston is here, my lady," he said under his breath. "Should I tell him to return later?"

Lillith's stomach clenched into a tight knot. The timing was horrendous, but before she could say anything, Victor appeared, coming up the steps.

"I couldn't wait," he said, his smile devastating to her senses.

She almost forgot her sister stood in the room behind her and would not understand, or perhaps she *would* understand all too well what Victor's presence meant, especially since she'd just been asking about him and now he magically appeared in her home.

He must have understood her hesitation, because his gaze skipped beyond her shoulder at the same moment Lillith felt her sister move directly behind her.

Victor glanced at Lillith, then back to Loraine. "Lady Melton, I presume."

Loraine actually scowled. "Yes, and you are?"

Dear God, she could be embarrassing when she wanted to be.

"I am Lord Graston, but please, call me Victor since we will be family very soon."

Lillith watched the emotions play over her sister's face—shock, excitement, and then suspicion, all within the space of five seconds.

"Please, won't you join us?" Lillith said, before asking Edward to bring them tea and shutting the door behind him.

As Victor moved farther into the room, Loraine watched him, her gaze assessing, taking in everything. Lillith felt herself bristle. Could she be more bold? The two of them had had a strange rivalry throughout the years, and Loraine had always used her outgoing personality to win over suitors, even those who might have shown interest in Lillith to begin with. It felt like one of those times all over again.

"So you are brother to my future son-in-law," Loraine said, winning smile in place. She licked her lips lazily and glanced at Lillith.

Lillith smiled softly, hoping her sister couldn't read the truth all over her face.

"Yes, I am, and might I say how thrilled I am that your lovely daughter will be joining my family. I could not have found a better match for my brother."

"Please, do sit down, Lord Graston," Lillith said, knowing her sister was gauging every last detail of the exchange.

"I merely dropped by to tell you that I heard from Sinjin just this morning, so it is quite fortunate that you are here, Lady Melton, for I wished to share the news with Katelyn's aunt, and now I can share it with you as well."

Loraine perked up immediately, acting the doting mother once more. "What is it?"

"Sinjin is returning to London tonight."

Loraine clapped her hands together. "That is wonderful news, indeed. Katelyn shall be elated."

"Thank you for bringing us word," Lillith murmured. "I look forward to seeing your brother again."

"Thank you, Lady Nordland," he said, his gaze shifting to the low neckline of her gown. Lillith very nearly tugged at it but refrained.

"Well, I will not interrupt your visit further," Victor said, moving toward the door. "I do so hope to see you both in the very near future."

Loraine beamed. "I shall look forward to it, Lord Graston."

Lillith wished her sister would leave already, but she did not budge as Victor nodded and left.

He let himself out, and only when the door closed did Loraine turn to look at Lillith. "Well, he certainly is a handsome man."

Her stomach tightened. "Yes, he is."

"Does Sinjin look anything like him?"

"Yes, they have the same eyes, the same thick, dark hair, but Sinjin's hair is straighter. The youngest is . . . well, breathtaking, to be sure."

"Victor was breathtaking, if you ask me."

The comment pleased Lillith and she smiled to herself.

"You think so, too, don't you?" Loraine asked, a wide, knowing grin on her lips.

"I think you would have to be dead, or insane, not to think him breathtakingly handsome."

"I am surprised he came by your townhouse. Tell me, how does he even know where you live?"

"I must have told him."

"How very fascinating." Loraine lifted both brows and pressed her hands to her waist.

"He is very kind."

"Yes, and perhaps interested in you."

She swallowed past the lump in her throat. "Do not be silly, Loraine. As he said, we are to be family soon, and he only wished to share the news of Sinjin's return with me so that I could tell Katelyn."

Loraine's lips quirked. "Believe what you will, dear sister, but that man wants you. Just be careful. I do not want to see you get hurt."

The words were like a sharp slap across the cheek. "Why would I be hurt?"

"Younger men are known for their liaisons. There has been many a widow who has been taken in by a young man's pretty face, only to be sorry when he has robbed her blind later."

"Yes, you would know firsthand, would you not?" The words were out before she could recant them.

Loraine's eyes narrowed. "Oh dear, I have hit a nerve, I see."

"No, I am simply stating the truth. You yourself are involved with a much younger man. Are you afraid of being hurt, or rather, robbed blind?"

Loraine snorted as though the very idea Anthony would rob her blind was ludicrous. "Anthony is hardly in the same category as Lord Graston, my dear. He is grateful, to say the least, and not about to give up a good thing. He can hardly rob me blind, as I don't have a lot of money. Whereas your Lord Graston is in high demand with all the debutantes. I can see why he would be interested in a widow. Some men prefer experience over youth."

Lillith's nails dug into her palms. She was reminded every day that Lady Rochester expected all her sons to marry young, eligible women, and soon. Lillith had proved to be a diversion for Victor, that is all. No more, no less, and she could not get her hopes up too high in that regard. It would be foolish to do so. "Well, whatever the case, I am glad you have found a companion, Loraine."

Loraine smiled genuinely for the first time since arriving. "Thank you. I appreciate your well wishes." She folded her hands before her. "And I hope that you find happiness, too, dear sister. I know you have not always had an easy time of it."

If only they had the type of relationship where she could share her innermost thoughts, then she most certainly would be more forthcoming about Victor, but she would not go there. She would never tell Loraine every delicious detail about her relationship with Victor, despite how much she yearned to.

"You desire him. I see it in your eyes."

Lillith dropped her gaze. "As you said, he is breathtaking, and it is hard, if not impossible, not to become tongue-tied when in his presence."

"We must find you a lover."

Those were the exact same words Janet had said to her the night after attending the hideaway club.

"Perhaps one day."

Loraine's eyes lit up. "That's the spirit," she said, patting Lillith on the back. "A lover is exactly what you need. And speaking of lovers, I must get back to Anthony. He becomes impatient when I am gone for too long."

Victor eyed the gown through the storefront window. He could already envision Lillith draped in the lovely emerald silk with its fine detailed gold stitching. Perhaps he would buy her a hat and shoes to match.

He had gone by her townhouse, wanting to see her, wanting to take her shopping, but her sister's visit had stopped any hope of that. He had seen the look of alarm in Lillith's eyes when he'd appeared. Apparently she did not want anyone knowing about them.

Up to this point they had kept their relationship a secret, but for how long? He wanted to take her out, show her the sights and spoil her beyond reason. He had not considered that perhaps she did not want to be seen with him, a man with a sordid reputation and she a woman known for her virtue.

It was all very sobering to think that might be the case. Undeterred by his thoughts, he stepped into the dressmaker's.

Lady Dante, who was no lady at all, came at him in a flurry of pink satin and a veritable cloud of rose perfume. "Lord Graston, how lovely to see you again."

He was stunned she remembered his name, as he had been in her shop on only a handful of occasions.

"Thank you, Lady Dante," he replied, kissing the hand she extended. Even her hands reeked of roses. Did the woman bathe in it, for goodness sake?

"What can I interest you in today, my lord?" she asked, glancing toward the store window. "Could I have my girl get the gown you were just looking at down for you?"

"Yes."

She lifted a whistle from the ribbon about her neck and blew. It was not a high, shrill ring, and Victor wondered why she could not have gained the girl's attention in some other way.

"Shannon, there you are. Are you deaf, girl?" she said, shaking her head in exasperation.

Shannon was not very old, maybe seventeen, with large, ice blue eyes and light blond hair. She was pale and looked extremely frail.

"Lord Graston would like to see the dress. Please take it off the mannequin and try it on."

"Yes, ma'am. Right away," the girl murmured.

"No, she does not need to try it on. If it does not fit, I can have it returned, correct?"

"Does the woman live here in London?"

"Yes."

"Then I can come to her if she wishes not to come to the shop. I understand these matters."

No doubt she did. She clothed three quarters of the mistresses in London.

The girl had the gown off the mannequin in record time and handed it to Victor with a curtsy.

The gown truly was exquisite, the detail impeccable. "Will you have it boxed up for me?"

Lady Dante beamed. "Of course, my lord. Would you like it delivered?"

"Yes," he said, giving her Lily's address.

"Very well, my lord. Shannon, please box up the gown. Shall I put this on your account?"

"Yes, thank you."

The bell above the door rang and Lady Dante didn't break eye contact with him.

"Victor, what a surprise."

Victor's blood turned cold. It was Selene.

Lady Dante's gaze shifted between the two of them.

Selene wore a pale pink evening gown that showed her attributes to absolute perfection. She looked ready for a ball rather than a day of shopping.

He managed a smile. "Selene, what a surprise."

Lady Dante backed away, smile still in place.

"What are you up to, Vicky?" she asked playfully, looking beyond his shoulder, no doubt scanning the shop for his companion.

"Shopping," he replied, heading for the door.

Her eyes widened. "You have found a bride. Well, let me be the first to offer my congratulations."

"I am not engaged, Selene."

Her lips quirked. "Ah, I see. Well, apparently some lucky woman has gained your favor. If memory serves, I could barely interest you in darkening the door of any dressmakers. She must be extremely special."

He wasn't about to bite. He didn't trust Selene as far as he could throw her.

"And what of you—are you here to spend some of the count's hard-earned money?"

She swallowed hard, her smile faltering as she leaned forward. "I am leaving him, Victor."

"I am sorry to hear that."

Her brows furrowed. "I made a mistake, Victor. A huge mistake. I want you."

Oddly, he felt nothing as he stared into her brown eyes. She had disappointed him greatly when he'd discovered her cheating ways, but her infidelity had honestly been one of the best things that had ever happened to him. "What we had is over, Selene."

Selene's agitation was obvious. "Who is the dress for?"

"A friend," he said, starting for the door.

"Do not tell me you are still seeing the widow."

He nearly missed a step. He knew Selene and didn't trust her for a moment not to shout the truth to anyone who would listen. Personally, he did not care if others discovered that Lillith was his lover, but he knew Lillith would care. "Who I see is none of your business."

She lifted her chin and managed a pretty smile. "It was nice to see you, Victor. I hope to see you, and your little widow, very soon."

14

A knock sounded at the front door as Lillith was making her way to her bedchamber to change for the evening. She stopped midstep. She was not in the mood for any more visitors this afternoon . . . well, unless that visitor was Victor Rayborne.

She had hoped he would stop back by, but as the day progressed she had started to lose hope.

She opened the door and a young girl stared back at her from a face as perfect as a doll's. Her pale blond hair was tied back in a simple braid, emphasizing her beautiful bone structure. Her almond-shaped eyes were truly amazing. They were ice blue and reminded her of a wolf's eyes. She was painfully thin, the plain dress hanging from her skinny body. And was that a bruise on her cheek?

"Lady Nordland?"

"Yes," Lillith replied, realizing how rude she'd been by staring at the girl in such a way.

"Oh," she said, no doubt surprised to have her answering the door. "I have a delivery for you."

Edward came up from behind Lillith, and she smiled and motioned him away.

"My lady, are you certain?" he queried, but with a reassuring glance from Lillith he backed away from the door. Lillith knew he would linger just in case he was needed.

The girl motioned to a young man who was in the seat of a Highflyer phaeton pulled by two white horses. It was obvious the two were siblings, their looks so similar. The boy was taller than the girl, but he had the same unique eyes.

"This is a delivery from Lady Dante's dressmakers," the girl said with a hint of an accent that Lillith could not pin down.

"I believe you have the wrong address, my dear."

Her brows furrowed and she glanced at the number on the townhouse, then at the sheet of paper in hand. "You are Lady Nordland, correct?"

"Yes, I am."

"This is a gift for you," the boy said, but clamped his mouth shut when his sister elbowed him.

A gift. She could not recall the last time she had received a present. Lillith took the large box from the boy and smiled. The two started down the stairs. "How long have you worked for Lady Dante?"

"A few weeks," the boy said, and Lillith once again detected the slightest hint of an accent.

"Where do you live, if you do not mind me asking?" she inquired, feeling moved to do so by the state of the girl's frail health.

"At the store, my lady," the boy said, shifting on his feet.

The girl reached out and grabbed his arm, as though she was worried he'd said too much already.

"Do you have time for a cup of tea?" Lillith asked.

"We must go," the girl said matter-of-factly, but Lillith could tell by the boy's hesitation that he wanted to come in.

"Please, just for a few minutes. I mean you no harm."

The boy glanced at the girl, and she sighed heavily and motioned him forward. Lillith turned and headed inside, passing by Edward, who smiled softly.

"Tea for three, my lady?"

"Yes, Edward, thank you. We shall be in the parlor."

Lillith sat down on a settee, placing the box beside her.

"Please, have a seat," she said, pointing to the two chairs nearest the fire.

The two sat down and Lillith looked from one to the other. They were so young. Too young to be on their own. Where was their mother, for goodness sake? Certainly they had family somewhere who missed them. "My name is Lillith."

"I am Shannon, and this is my brother, Zachary."

"It is nice to meet you both."

They looked around the parlor, taking everything in. Shannon folded her hands in her lap, her shoulders rigid, chin lifted high.

Edward entered the parlor with a silver tray, a pot of tea, and three cups. He poured them each a cup, and asked if they desired cream and sugar. Cook arrived a moment later with a plateful of cookies.

Zachary's eyes lit up.

"Are you going to open the box?" Shannon asked in an excited voice.

"Of course." Lillith untied the ribbon and lifted the top off. Her breath caught in her throat. It was a beautiful emerald gown with exquisite gold adornments.

Her hands shook as she pulled the gown from the tissue. It looked like a perfect fit, and she could hardly wait to try it on.

"It's lovely. The finest in the store, my lady."

"Aye," Zachary agreed, stuffing another cookie into his mouth.

His sister scowled at him, and he pressed the napkin to his lips.

"Indeed, it is."

"The gentleman said it would be perfect for you."

She could imagine Victor picking it out, and her heart swelled with affection for him. She felt like the luckiest woman in the world.

She set the dress aside, then lifted her cup and took a sip, all the while watching the two.

"So, tell me, what are your plans for the future? Do you desire to be a dressmaker or seamstress, is that why you work for Lady Dante?"

"No, I do not wish to be a dressmaker or seamstress," Shannon replied matter-of-factly. "She had a sign in her window that said HELP WANTED, and it worked out since we were new to the city and were looking for work."

"You are from Ireland?"

"We are not from Ireland," the boy blurted, and Lillith realized she had struck a nerve. Again, she wondered at their circumstance.

"Oh, I am sorry, I thought I detected an accent."

"We are from . . . Scotland," the boy said.

"Where about?" Lillith asked.

"Inverness," the girl said at the same time the boy said, "Edinburgh."

Lillith definitely knew they were hiding something now. "So, tell me, are you paid well by Lady Dante?"

"We work for room and board."

"And nothing else?" Lillith said, horrified that the dressmaker was taking such advantage of the two.

Zachary set his now-empty cup down. "I wash dishes at Watiers' each night for extra money."

Lillith knew the gentleman's club well. It had been a favorite of her husband's.

"And do you work another job?" Lillith asked Shannon, almost afraid of the answer.

"No, Zachary does not want me to."

"I only run errands, but Shannon sews all day and night, and even goes on deliveries when the shop slows down. One job is enough." He glanced toward the clock on the mantel and leaned forward.

"What if I told you that I am looking for a maid and a footman," Lillith said.

The siblings looked at each other, and Lillith could see hope in their eyes. "What do the positions pay?" Shannon asked.

"I pay forty pounds a year, paid quarterly, and you shall each have Sunday off to do as you wish."

Zachary's eyes widened.

"Thank you, Lady Nordland," Shannon said, casting an excited glance in her brother's direction.

Edward appeared at the door. "Lord Graston is here, my lady."

Lillith's heart gave a jolt. "Please, have him come in."

She heard Victor take the steps two at a time. His smile faltered when he looked at Zachary, then Shannon. "Well, I see my gift has arrived."

"Yes, it is lovely," Lillith said, standing to greet him.

Zachary cleared his throat and Shannon stood. "We should be going. Thank you for the tea and cookies, my lady."

"Do let me know what you decide." Lillith said, walking them to the door.

She rushed back up the steps and Victor was standing at the window. "You are taking them on as servants?" he asked, his smile saying he was pleased.

"Something is not right with their story, I fear, but I will not push them."

"You are kind and thoughtful," he said, and she flushed.

"It is you who are kind." She went to the box, lifted the dress, and put it up to her.

The dress was exquisite and Lillith could not keep the smile from her face. Victor sat in a chair, grinning boyishly as she stepped up to the mirror and admired her reflection.

"The color matches your eyes perfectly."

And it did. "It's beautiful, Victor." Any further words stuck in her throat. In all the years she'd been married, Winfred had never spoiled her with gifts. "Thank you so much. I cannot wait to wear it."

He looked pleased by her reaction. "Wear it tonight."

"I am not going out tonight." She had declined an invitation to a soiree, and she hated to be seen somewhere else and word return to the person who had invited her.

"Come with me, Lillith. Please."

How could she deny him? How handsome he was dressed in his expensive black suit with dove gray waistcoat, his long legs crossed at the ankle.

"Where are we going?"

"Anywhere."

He wanted to take her out in public.

His eyes narrowed the slightest bit. "You hesitate, Lily. Are you ashamed of me?"

She lifted her brows. "How could you think that?"

"Then prove me wrong and come with me. Let me take you out, wear your new gown, and let us experience all this city has to offer."

He unfurled himself from the chair and approached her, coming behind her and wrapping her in his strong embrace. She loved the feel of being in his arms, and smiled at the image in the mirror. She did not see a mature woman with a young man but rather an attractive couple who complemented each other.

"Come with me, Lily."

She smiled at him in the mirror. "Yes."

15

The smells of the city rose up to greet Lillith as the carriage rolled along the busy streets.

The park was alive with activity, and she smiled at a woman rushing after two children. Nearby, a young man and woman sat on a blanket, the woman reading from a book, the man watching her with open adoration.

Beside her, Victor shifted, and she glanced at him. He was watching her, and the sides of his mouth lifted in a warm grin, his blue eyes sparkling.

God's truth, she could not recall a time she had been so happy, and it was all because of him. He made her so excited about life, made her yearn for what the future had in store. She smoothed out the skirts of her new gown and returned his smile. "Where are we going?"

"To one of my favorite places in London."

Lillith realized how very little she knew about Victor when they pulled up to a small restaurant in Covent Garden. She could feel the stares of those who were less fortunate gather around them as they stopped to watch Victor help her from the carriage.

Victor placed a hand on her hip and walked her inside the restaurant. The interior was dark, with only a handful of booths. Many of the diners stared but quickly went back to eating or drinking. An old man with thick gray hair, a mustache, and a large nose beamed when he saw Victor. "Vicky," he said, his arms spread wide as he came forward. "How are you doing, my boy?"

"I am well, Alessandro," he said, shaking his hand. "I have brought my good friend to dine at your establishment."

"Well, I am honored. Please, have a seat," he said, motioning toward a large table in the very back of the room.

The chair creaked when Lillith sat down. The table had thick scratches all over its surface, and the walls had been painted with a charming mural of an Italian village.

"What do you think?" Victor asked.

"It is different."

He laughed under his breath, and she felt heat race up her cheeks. All her life she had been brought up in privilege, never entering establishments such as this one.

And it was difficult to remember that Victor, too, had been brought up in a similar fashion, and yet from the way he had been greeted, it was obvious that he was familiar with the people and this place.

There was just so much she didn't know about him. "I am glad you brought me here, Victor."

Dinner was incredible—authentic Italian food and delectable bread that melted in her mouth. She washed it all down with a glass of red wine that warmed her insides.

She sat back in her creaky chair, pleasantly full.

Victor smiled at her and her pulse skittered. Already she

looked forward to the hours ahead. "Take me home," she said, not phrasing it as a question.

"Very well, my lady," he said, standing. Taking her hand within his large one, he led her toward the door.

Alessandro said good-bye, giving them both hugs, and Lillith left the restaurant feeling excited and liking very much what she had seen in Victor.

Inside the carriage, he pulled her toward him and kissed her.

He tasted of brandy and she smiled against his lips.

"Thank you for dinner."

"You are welcome, my dear. I am glad you enjoyed yourself."

"I did, indeed, though I fear I shall not eat for a week."

His blue eyes glittered as he stared at her, the smile slipping from his features. Her heart was not about to slow down anytime soon. He thrilled her, excited her in a way that made her feel ten years younger.

And he was full of surprises. Because of his reputation as a rakehell, she had assumed he was a pampered lord, and yet at every turn she was seeing another side to him, a refreshing side that made her yearn to experience his life.

"Did I tell you how beautiful you are tonight?" he said, and her thighs tightened as his gaze slipped to the low neckline of her gown.

"Yes, as a matter-of-fact, you did. But I shall never grow weary of hearing you say it."

His lips curved, flashing a wolfish smile that heated her blood. Desire swooped low into her belly, and her gaze slid to the noticeable bulge in his trousers. On impulse, she reached for him, her hands moving to the buttons of his trousers, and with surprising deftness, she reached for his cock.

His manhood was beautiful, and as her fingers slid over the

plum-sized head, a drop of moisture seeped from the slit. She licked her lips and lowered her head, taking him into her mouth.

A wondrous moan came from deep in his chest, and he leaned back against the velvet cushion, his hand moving to her shoulder, his thumb brushing over her collarbone.

She followed her instincts, taking him deeper into her mouth, while her hand slid around his thick base, fingers caressing his balls.

His size made it impossible to take him completely into her mouth, the crown hitting the back of her throat, but she sucked and laved him, her tongue teasing the ridge, dancing over the slit again and again.

His breathing became more labored, his hips flexing against her mouth.

He reached beneath her skirts, pulling her gown up, touching her slick entrance. Seconds later, she was lifted onto his lap and he impaled her, his impossibly hard cock buried deep in her moist heat.

They sighed in unison, and Lillith knew she'd never forget the sound. She rode him slow and steady at first, but with every turn of the carriage wheel, she quickened her pace, frantic to finish before they returned to his townhouse.

Her nails curled around the seat back. His hands were planted on her hips, but he didn't try to take control. She finally slowed down, adjusting the position to where the head of his cock brushed her sensitive spot, arching her back just so.

He cupped her breasts with both hands, bringing them out of their confines with a quick movement, his thumbs circling her areolas, plucking at them.

Then he bent his head and took one into his mouth. Looking down at him, she watched in wonder as his tongue teased one bud, then the other. It was so erotic to watch him pleasure her. With every swipe of his tongue, she grew wetter.

His dark hair teased her arms, and she ran her fingers through the silky tresses, her nails digging into his scalp.

Exhilaration licked her spine as Victor used his teeth with just the right amount of restraint.

She felt absolutely scandalous knowing that a tiny sliver of fabric was all that separated her from the outside world they were passing by. A sliver away from discovery. She would have never dared anything so brazen before, but Victor brought out the wanton in her, and she liked it. Enjoyed the sense of impropriety for the first time in her life.

Seconds away from orgasm, she looked into his eyes and her breath left her in a rush. His expression was positively smoldering, his eyes heavy lidded and dark. The sides of his mouth lifted along with a thrust of his hips and her world exploded, shattering into a thousand pieces.

Selene sat in the unmarked carriage across from Victor's townhouse. She had sent a boy up to the estate, saying he had a message for Victor, and Jeffries had answered. The boy had returned saying Lord Graston was out for a few hours. Rory had come home a short time ago with a beautiful young woman on his arm who resembled the wife of a wealthy viscount. They had departed not even an hour later looking flushed and well sated.

Now Selene waited expectantly, hoping that Howard would not show up at her flat looking for her.

She nearly gave up waiting when the familiar black carriage with the Rochester crest pulled up to the townhouse.

Her heart raced in anticipation. She tugged at the bodice of her new gown, similar in cut to the one Victor had bought Lady

Nordland, but hopefully different enough that he would not know she had bought it on purpose. Beneath her gown she wore nothing save for black stockings that tied at the thigh with a red ribbon. Already she could envision letting the gown fall to her feet in a puddle of silk wearing nothing but a smile.

The sex would be incredible. She craved Victor's big cock and the pleasure he could give her. A pleasure no one else could touch. She wiggled in anticipation.

She would wait several minutes after Victor entered the townhouse to send the boy around again. After all, she didn't want to appear to be following him.

The driver stepped down from the carriage and lowered the steps. He opened the door, then lifted a hand to help someone down.

Selene's stomach fell when a familiar blonde took the servant's hand and walked down the two steps, followed by Victor. His dark hair was tousled, and he was grinning widely as he put a hand on the widow's slender back. She was wearing the beautiful gown she had seen in Lady Dante's storefront.

Piercing jealousy washed over Selene and she swallowed bitter disappointment. Damn the bitch! Her agitation only grew by leaps and bounds when Lady Nordland looked up at Victor with a warm smile, her slender hand slipping around his bulging bicep.

They looked like any happy couple, content, laughing. She could not recall a single time she had been that happy with Howard. Her count was far too serious, with no sense of humor to speak of, and his idea of an enjoyable evening was playing cards and drinking brandy.

She remembered Victor, how he had treated her like a princess, taking her to the finest restaurants, to the opera, and anywhere she desired. And she had been so incredibly proud to be with a man whom so many women desired. What a bloody fool she was for taking it all for granted.

Now Lady Nordland must be savoring being the object of his affection, and the envy of every woman in London. How shocked many would be to learn the widow was not so respectable anymore.

Victor and Lady Nordland walked up the steps, and Selene wanted to scream her agitation for him to hear. What on earth was he thinking? Did he actually desire the woman? She had heard on good authority she was barren. After all, had she not been married for upward of twenty years and still had no children? Certainly Lord and Lady Rochester would never stand for such a union.

Selene had once asked Victor if he desired children, and he had said that he had. Had that changed all the sudden?

Or perhaps she was getting ahead of herself. Victor probably just wanted to fuck the woman; then he would toss her aside like all the others. He loved the pursuit . . . just as he had pursued her.

And the chase had been most exhilarating.

And now she would pursue him with pure abandon. Nothing would stand in her way, especially an aging, childless widow.

Misgivings ate at her. Victor rarely brought women to the family home. And to do so this early in the evening meant only one thing.

Her insides twisted in a painful knot.

Lady Nordland had absolutely no ties—no children, no husband, no lover. She was free to come and go as she pleased, and apparently, if she was out in the open with Victor, she was not keeping the affair hidden.

Selene watched with sinking despair as the door closed shut behind them.

Her nails dug into her skin as her gaze shifted to the window of Victor's room. It was foolish to sit and watch, to wait, and yet she could not bring herself to leave.

Only a minute or two passed when the drapes at Victor's upstairs window shifted. Seconds later, she saw the tall silhouette. It was Victor, and he was looking over at someone, his white teeth flashing in his tanned face; then he closed the drapes.

She wrapped on the carriage window with more force than necessary and the driver appeared at the door a second later. "Are ye ready to leave, madam, or should I fetch the boy again?"

His face was impassive, but she swore she saw sympathy in his eyes.

Selene lifted her chin. "No, please just take me home."

"Very well, madam," he said with a nod.

The carriage shifted once again beneath his weight as he settled in the seat. Her plans, along with hope for a reunion, withered away.

16

The hotel ballroom was filled to capacity, and Lillith was relieved when a servant dressed in a black velvet jacket and powdered wig opened several of the windows, allowing the brisk night air into the stifling room.

She took in the splendor of the room—the eight large chandeliers overhead, and the minimal decorations in lovely shades of primrose, blues, and mauves.

She had once again worn the gown that Victor had given her, and her new maid, the lovely Shannon, had artfully fixed her hair into a series of curls that flattered her face.

It was wonderful to have Janet with her. They had finally spoken at length about the hideaway visit, and Janet apologized, saying she felt horrible that she had taken Lillith to such a place. Lillith had taken responsibility for accepting, and they had promised each other to not speak of it ever again.

"There is a woman staring at you," Janet said, and Lillith followed her line of vision.

Her stomach nearly fell to her feet. Selene MacLeod watched her from across the room, that now-familiar smirk on her lips.

The young actress held her gaze for a few seconds and Lillith clearly read a challenge there.

Lillith scanned the room, looking for the count. Certainly she wouldn't be here alone . . . or would she?

"That is Victor's ex-mistress."

"Ah," Janet said, dark brows lifted.

Lillith had finally told her old friend about Victor. Janet had clapped her hands in delight and asked for very specific details. Though Lillith had answered nearly every question, she found she could not be too forthcoming about all she had shared with Victor. Janet told her how very happy she was, especially when Lillith told her she had never felt so alive and happy.

He thrilled her senses, made her feel like a woman, appreciated and extremely desired, and she was falling harder for him by the day.

"Do not concern yourself with Miss MacLeod. I will take care of her," Janet said sternly, and Lillith believed her.

Victor had invited Lillith to the soiree, but she had already made plans to come with her friend. He had agreed to meet her here, and Lillith worried about his reaction to seeing Selene.

Just four nights ago Lillith and Victor had had their first official outing, and he had not hidden from anyone, but nor had she. People were already talking. She could see the smiles, the snickers behind fans, but they could all be damned. And tonight, all of her peers would know the truth, because she would not hide behind closed doors any longer.

She had found a new lease on life, and she wouldn't trade places with anyone for the world.

Janet glanced toward Selene. "I swear if she does not quit staring at you, I am afraid I am going to have to pull her outside."

"I am not afraid of her."

As Janet stared at Selene, she made an expression that resembled a child who had taken a drink of spoiled milk. "I wonder just how many of these husbands she has slept with."

Lillith's eyes widened and Janet laughed under her breath. "What? You think I am being harsh considering my reputation. Well, I'll have you know that I make it a point to never dally with another woman's husband. I would hate the same to come back on me one day."

Pleasantly surprised by the statement, Lillith nodded. "I have seen her often this past week."

"Your paths usually do not cross, I take it?"

"Correct." Even more disturbing was the fact that Selene always appeared to be alone. "I did not tell you that she came to Claymoore Hall the final night I was there."

"Oh dear," Janet said, taking a glass off a passing waiter's tray. "Was she there to beg for her lover back?"

"Yes, and what's more, everyone sensed her desperation. I have been in those shoes before." Lillith said this last almost absently.

"So I am assuming it was Victor who called a stop to the affair?"

"I do not know the specifics, nor do I want to."

"Wait a second—isn't she the mistress of Count de Lamonde?"

"Yes."

Janet's eyes lit up. "I understand the poor countess is beside herself with worry, for her husband has never before been so taken with one of his lovers. He attends nearly every one of her performances, and it is common knowledge he visits her dressing room right before she goes on and has her," she said, wiggling her bows.

"Surely you jest?"

"No, I do not. Every single time, and everyone in the theater knows it, and the count likes it that way. Apparently, he is terrified of losing her. Anyway, I do believe the countess fears he may divorce her."

Now that was shocking. Lillith knew many men who had been pressured into marriage by mistresses, but nine times out of ten the man never went through with a divorce. It was too difficult to get, too expensive, and too devastating to the families involved. "Is the count here?"

"No, though I am surprised, given what a tight leash he keeps the little actress on," Janet said, pursing her lips. "I do not see him here tonight, but I do see someone else."

Lillith followed her gaze and her heart tripped seeing Victor coming toward her. He looked gorgeous dressed in black trousers tucked into polished Hessians, a charcoal gray waistcoat, and a navy jacket that made his eyes even more brilliant.

"Oh my goodness, he is absolutely lovely, Lily." Janet's voice was breathless, her gaze appreciative as she watched his approach. She released a tiny gasp. "He is even more handsome than the last time I saw him. Oh, and that must be little brother."

Rory followed behind Victor. "Why, yes, it is."

Lillith could certainly appreciate her friend's reaction to Rory, but honestly, she found Victor the most beautiful and charming of the three brothers.

"You are a lucky lady, my friend," Janet whispered.

Lillith did feel lucky, and excited for the future for the first time in what seemed like forever.

He smiled at her, and his gaze skipped to just beyond her shoulder, in the direction of Selene. To his credit, his gaze remained impassive, and Lillith would have given anything to know his thoughts. Jealousy was an emotion she was well acquainted with from the years of her marriage, and that depressing emotion reared its ugly head now and reminded her yet again of the differences between herself and Victor's ex-mistress.

"Hello, Lady Nordland," he said, lifting her hand and kissing the tips of her fingers.

She was reminded of the scandalous carriage ride through the streets of London, of the sound of their moans mingling as she rode him, of the hours after as they had made love and lay in each others' arms. She had returned to her home completely sated and walking on air.

"This is my friend, Janet Rencourt."

"I have heard much about you, Mrs. Rencourt," Victor said, kissing Janet's hand.

Her friend glanced at Lillith and they shared a smile.

Rory was introduced next, and Janet was soon gushing and stumbling over her words. Lillith wondered what it must be like to have people react to you in such a way.

"You look lovely, Lily," Victor murmured, his hand moving to her hip. She could feel heat rush up her neck. She had never been one to blush, but he brought out the girl in her, and she knew others stared. *Let them judge,* she thought. Ironically, she realized how little she was starting to care about what others thought of her.

"Thank you, and you are very handsome, my lord."

"You delight me," he said, and the words gave her a little shiver. Already she yearned to be in his arms and share his bed.

Rory and Janet seemed to be hitting it off, and Lillith grinned to herself, wondering if her friend might very well be going home with the young Rayborne, who was known to dally with women of all ages. Perhaps they would pass each other in the hall come morning.

Selene approached them, her expensive perfume nearly taking one's breath away. She truly was stunning, flawless in every way, her complexion perfect, her lips rouged a bright red, and her dark hair swept up off her elegant neck.

Lillith swallowed hard and tried with difficulty not to feel inadequate.

She felt Victor stiffen beside her, and he even pulled Lillith closer.

"Good evening," Selene said, her gaze skipping over Lillith before focusing on Victor.

He gave a curt nod.

"May I have a word with you?"

His brows furrowed. "We have nothing to talk about."

Selene licked her lips and had the grace to look embarrassed. "It will only take a moment."

"It cannot wait?"

She shook her head.

"Will you excuse me?" Victor asked Lillith, his tone apologetic.

Lillith forced a smile. "Yes, of course."

She watched the two walk toward one set of double doors that led out to the verandah.

Thank goodness the dancing started, and couples filed out onto the floor. Laughter and talking ensued, the music nearly drowning out all effort at conversation. But Rory did his best to keep Lillith occupied; it was difficult, though, when her thoughts were with Victor.

What was Selene up to, and why had she chosen such a public venue to talk with him? Had it been on purpose?

Lillith had been to the hotel on several occasions for various events, so she was familiar with the floorplan. If she went to the second level, she could look down onto the verandah.

Yet, as much as her curiosity begged her to check on the two, she put the thought far from her mind. She would not resort to the acts of a jealous mistress. Could she even be considered a mistress, or was she merely his lover? How did one know or differentiate?

She tightened her fists at her sides. No, she had to trust Victor, and from her earlier interactions with Selene, Lillith knew he did not ask for the woman's attention or affection. She was more of an irritant, and he had let her know it at every turn.

Her gaze caught and held Janet's, and Lillith felt her flush deepen as she saw sympathy and concern in her friend's eyes.

Victor counted to ten twice. Selene did her best impression of a wounded lover, her brown eyes misting over as she watched him through lowered lashes. "I want to be with you, Victor, and no one else. I swear to you that I will be true."

Victor felt like he was in a bad dream that kept replaying. Why did she not understand him when he said he didn't want to be with her? How much more plainly could he put it?

"I made a mistake, and I will spend the rest of my life making it up to you."

He was growing weary of this game. "Selene, I am confused. You are the mistress of Count de Lamonde, who is extremely happy with you. You have everything you've always desired. What we had is now over. Forget about me, and enjoy your life."

"I only want you."

Victor ran a hand through his hair, exasperated beyond measure. "Jeffries said you dropped by the townhouse today. I would ask that you do not do so in the future."

Her gaze slid to his lips. "I wanted to talk to you. I didn't mean any harm. I was desperate."

"Well, we have talked, so there is no need for you to come to my parents' home."

"And yet you can bring a widow to their home and you think nothing of it."

He frowned. "You are following me now?"

She swallowed hard and he knew she had been watching the townhouse. How long had she been doing so? he wondered, worrying about Lillith's safety.

She licked her rouged lips, then glanced at the large windows into the ballroom where couples mingled, among them the woman he wanted to be with. "Come, step into the shadows with me."

"No." It was enough that he had walked outside with her.

Growing impatient, he cleared his throat. "Leave me alone, Selene. We have nothing more to discuss."

She grabbed his hand, her fingers curling around his. "I am pregnant, Victor. I am going to have your child."

The words stopped him cold. They had not been intimate for weeks now, but he knew a woman could hide a pregnancy rather easily. Hadn't Rory just commented how she looked heavier than the last time he had seen her? He swallowed hard, his mind racing. "I would assume your count might be the father, along with a good number of other men."

"No, it was you. Remember that night at Dartmouth. The house party where you slipped into my room and we made love."

He had been extremely drunk. So drunk he could have forgotten about using protection. That night had been when he'd found out about the count, who was also at the party with his wife. Victor had gone with the intention of breaking it off with her, but he made a mistake in stopping at an inn en route to the party and getting pissed out of his mind.

He glanced at her stomach. "You do not look to be increasing."

She pressed her lips together. "I have been hiding my pregnancy for obvious reasons. Did you not wonder why I was only acting one night a week?"

He had heard the count didn't want her working at the theater because of his intense jealousy, not that she was pregnant.

Bloody hell, now this was a predicament. He had always been careful with all of his lovers, normally using condoms or pulling out to avoid just such a disaster. But that particular night he'd been too drunk to even remember how the night played out.

How dreadful.

The door opened and Rory appeared. "Is everything all right out here?" he asked, looking directly at Victor.

Victor nodded, "I'll be right there."

"The count just arrived," he said, and Victor could already envision the Frenchman scouring the room looking for his mistress.

"The countess is here too."

Selene sighed heavily.

Rory walked back into the room but did not close the door all the way. "I must return," Victor said, wishing he could go back to that night at Dartmouth. He wouldn't have left the inn, or better yet, his home.

"I shall contact you later to further discuss this matter."

Before he could respond, she rushed back into the room, and Victor stood out on the verandah for a long moment, his mind racing.

What a nightmare.

It made more sense that the child would belong to the count than Victor. Was Selene trying to stick Victor with the paternity because Howard was married and the child would be a bastard? It didn't seem too big a leap considering she'd come to Claymoore Hall the instant she'd heard he and his brothers were looking for brides.

All the excitement he'd felt for the night ahead faded in the face of reality. The news couldn't have come at a worse time, especially since he was having such a great time getting to know Lillith.

Lillith . . . whom he had promised never to hurt.

17

Rory felt every one of the ten glasses of whiskey he'd downed at the gentleman's bar before coming home. Poor Victor had revealed to him the devastating news about Selene's pregnancy earlier in the night. To be honest, Rory didn't believe the bitch for a minute, especially since she'd been fucking the count, among others, for months now. Like Victor said, she was no doubt looking for a husband and father for her child so neither one of them would be cast out by a jealous wife.

Tomorrow was another day. For now he was home, and thank goodness for that. Taking the steps two at a time, he was met by Jeffries, who took his hat, coat, and gloves. "Can I get you anything, my lord?"

"Is my brother home?"

"No."

Hopefully that meant he was with Lillith. Poor Lady Nordland, she would be gutted by the news.

Truth be told, he was surprised his brother and Lillith had continued their relationship beyond the party at Claymoore Hall. He had expected Victor to grow weary of her, and yet, he was taking their bet to heart. Apparently, he really wanted their grandfather's watch. That, or he was truly enamored of the lovely widow.

"There is a letter from your mother. I have placed it on your dresser."

"Thank you, Jeffries." Rory sighed. He had hoped now that Sinjin had found Katelyn that their mother would relent when it came to him and Victor. Already he hated the fact that he and his brothers could no longer dally at brothels or attend certain gentleman clubs together. After all, his brothers were his best mates.

It was not fun growing up.

He could not imagine himself as a husband, and the very thought of being a father terrified him. After all, what if he had sons who ended up like him?

He opened the door to his room and glanced at the letter sitting on the dresser.

Like any man, he adored his mother, but she really could be vexing at times.

A movement from the corner of his eye had him on alert, and he turned to find Lady Anna. Naked, she sat on a high-backed chair in a most arousing way, a pillow hiding her anatomy. Her blond hair was piled atop her head, tendrils caressing her shoulders.

His cock jerked to attention.

No wonder Jeffries had looked disconcerted. "I thought you were leaving for York?"

"London holds much more appeal at the moment."

It was a good thing he hadn't brought Lady Nordland's friend home tonight, else he would have been in a most unpleasant predicament.

Then again, given Lady Anna's love of the ménage à trois, she would have no doubt welcomed the other woman with open arms.

"I let myself in. Your valet nearly tackled me when I started up the stairs to your room, but I assured him that you would be pleased by my surprise."

Jeffries was lucky that was the case.

Rory untied his cravat, and slipped his shirt off with amazing speed and deftness for having been so tired moments before.

Anna tossed the pillow aside and his mouth went dry. She had shaved completely. She stood and walked toward him, her hips swaying in a most provocative way. "Let me help you with your boots."

She motioned for him to sit on the edge of the bed, then proceeded to turn, straddle his leg, and pull the boot off ever so slowly.

She had a lovely, slender back, and a pert little ass. By the time she removed the second boot, his cock was as hard as marble.

She turned and, with a wicked smile, began unbuttoning his trousers, sliding them to his ankles and then off.

Anna's gaze shifted to his cock. "Looks like you are happy to see me, after all."

Slowly, she went to her knees and took him into her mouth. He played with her nipples, teasing them into hard peaks.

He was so drunk that he would come quickly if she didn't slow down.

He pulled her up and she looked at him, clearly surprised. A sly smile played at her lips.

His hand moved to her soft belly, and over the cleanly shaven mons and hot flesh.

She was positively molten, and her inner muscles clenched his fingers as he pumped them in and out of her. She fondled his balls, caressing them in her palm, her fingers brushing the sensitive patch close to his rectum.

With a growl, he lifted her, and turning, rested her bottom on the edge of the bed. Her legs were spread impossibly wide as he entered her, and she leaned back on her hands, her breasts bobbing with each thrust.

The entire bed moved, screeching across the floor.

He watched as his length disappeared inside of her. She fell onto her back; her hand moved to her belly, over her shaved mound to her clit, her middle finger circling the tiny nub before adding another. With her other hand, she plucked at her nipple, hard, squeezing the bud, rolling it between finger and thumb.

She made a primal sound, her fingers working faster and faster; and then her sheath was contracting around him, drawing him in deeper as her climax milked him.

He lifted her legs over his shoulders, and shifted her slightly, sliding from her molten snatch, into her back passage. She moaned low, telling him without words how she loved it.

Legs shaking, he slowed his pace, sweat beading on his brow with each solid stroke. He brushed his thumb over her clit, over her hot, creamy entrance. He slipped two fingers inside, then another.

His fingers found her sweet spot inside her tight sheath, and she came again, coating his hand with her sweet juices.

He gripped her thighs tight, and with a final thrust, he came with a groan.

Everything was in place for Marilyn's coming-out ball, and Lillith just knew the night would be a success. She had worked tirelessly this past week on all the details, and she was confident that by year's end, both her nieces would be married off and on their ways to living out the rest of their lives in happiness.

At the soiree the other night she had been approached by the mother of another debutante who said she was having a coming out for her daughter, along with half a dozen other young women. She asked if Marilyn would like to join them, and Lillith had heartily agreed, but insisted on asking Marilyn first.

Marilyn had seemed excited, and said that she would rather be one of many versus having all the attention focused on her.

Lady Ashley had just left, and Marilyn looked over the guest list. So much had already been done that all they had to do was show up on the required date.

It would be a splendid affair.

And even more, Loraine said she would defer her plans to travel to Greece until after the ball.

Loraine walked in, as always an hour late for the meeting. "Lady Ashley just left."

"Oh, I'm so sorry to hear that," she said, looking completely unapologetic. "I tried to get away, but I fear I could not."

Lillith could not imagine what had been so important that she would miss a meeting about her daughter's coming-out ball. "Lady Ashley has left the guest list." Lillith handed it to Loraine. "Feel free to add any names."

"Did you wish to take Marilyn to the dressmaker's to start a gown, or would you like me to?"

"Go right ahead," Loraine said, smoothing a hand over her forehead. "You always had better taste in fashion than I did."

It was a rare compliment, but Lillith would take it. "Thank you."

"I'm sure she will be a vision, with your guidance." Loraine placed a hand over Lillith's.

In the past week Lillith had begun to understand her sister a little better. She realized how very much she missed that relationship in her life, and although her sister had not been the kind of mother that Lillith felt she should have been to Marilyn and Katelyn, she did care in her own way.

Perhaps in time their relationship would grow into the kind of bond she had always yearned to have with her sister.

"I wanted to speak to you about something," Loraine said, keeping her voice low.

Lillith lifted her brows, not sure what to expect. "Should I call for tea first?"

"No, this cannot wait."

Now she was curious.

Loraine cleared her throat and licked her lips. "There is no easy way for me to say this, so I will just come out with it."

Lillith's stomach clenched.

"I have heard it on good authority that Selene MacLeod is pregnant . . . and Victor is the father."

Lillith's heart nearly skittered to a stop. She waited for her sister to say she was joking, but she just looked at her without blinking.

"What makes you believe Victor is the father when Selene has been Count de Lamonde's mistress for months now?" Lillith asked, forcing the words past dry lips.

"Because someone I know very well overheard the conversation between Selene and Victor."

"No," Lillith said adamantly, "you misunderstood."

Loraine glanced at her, brows lifted high. "Lillith, I assure you my friend saw the two of them together at The Grand. They sat in a booth for nearly an hour, and then they left together. He dropped her off near the theater, and they kissed. I swear to you this is true."

Lillith felt physically sick.

"Perhaps your friend was mistaken. There are men aplenty in London who resemble Victor."

Loraine hugged her, and Lillith felt tears burn the backs of her eyes. "Lillith, Anthony knows what Victor looks like, and it was the Rochester crest on the side of his carriage. True, the brothers may all have similar characteristics, but it is easy to tell them apart even from a distance."

So . . . perhaps they had been together. But what did that prove really? Absolutely nothing, that's what. Plus, if Selene was pregnant, it stood to reason the baby belonged to the count and not Victor, right?

She thought back on this past week, of the couple of days she had seen Victor. Because of the plans with Marilyn's coming-out ball, she had not been available to see him every night, and when she did see him, he had seemed almost . . . distant and preoccupied. She had known the signs, had lived them with Winfred. He had become distant and aloof after the wedding, and she had learned soon enough why.

The betrayal felt familiar, and though Selene could have gotten pregnant before Lillith entered his life, it still didn't excuse the kiss or the private meetings that had taken place.

No wonder Selene had pulled him out onto the verandah at the soiree.

What a fool she was.

"What day did this take place exactly?" she asked, her voice sounding foreign and cold, even to her own ears.

Loraine brushed her top teeth over her bottom lip. "Tuesday, I believe."

Had Tuesday been the day he had been behaving oddly? She counted the days, and disappointment ate at her insides when she realized that on Tuesday he'd been extremely distracted. She had known that getting involved with a rakehell had its risks, but she had not expected for the liaison to end so quickly, especially when he had given her every indication he was pleased with her.

He sent flowers, chocolates, and just yesterday she had received a sapphire silk shawl.

No doubt out of guilt. Men were always good at giving gifts to the women they hurt.

"I wanted you to find out before he said anything, Lillith. I want you to be prepared." She put her at arm's length. "Do not show him that you are hurt."

Lillith actually saw sympathy in Loraine's eyes. "Look him square in the eye and tell him to never contact you again."

She closed her eyes and took a breath. She wanted to scream at the top of her lungs. She wanted to drink away her sorrows. She wanted to go to bed, sleep for a month, and when she woke, she wanted the pain to be gone.

"Do not let this detract you from taking other lovers, Lillith. Anthony has several friends, all of whom would be delighted to—"

"No," Lillith said, cutting off her sister. She could not even imagine getting involved with another man after Victor. He had been all that she desired, and no one else held any appeal whatsoever. "I need no help in finding a man, sister. I have lived this long and only taken one other man as a lover. I am old enough to make my own choices."

And she would stay single and alone for the rest of her life because she never wanted to be hurt like this again.

"Bravo," Loraine said, flashing a soft smile. "I am glad to hear it. It is long past due, I say. And I am shocked you are taking the news so well. I thought you might be devastated, for you seemed quite attached."

She just could not help herself, could she?

"Perhaps you will find a nice man one day. A quiet, studious man, who is not a womanizing scoundrel."

Yes, a man who would take care of her heart and not trounce

on it after making her fall deeply and passionately in love with him. A man who believed in honor and trust.

Silly, silly woman, she thought to herself. Why had she allowed herself to believe for even an instant that she could find happiness with Victor Rayborne?

Loraine walked to the sideboard, took down two tall crystal glasses, and filled them both to the rim with scotch. She managed to make it back to the table without spilling any. Handing one glass to Lillith, she lifted the other. "You shall come around, sister, and when you do, I shall take you by the hand and we shall have a delightful time."

Lillith forced a smile for her sister's benefit and took a long drink of the liquor, savoring the feel as it made a warm path down her throat to her stomach.

From across the room, Lillith saw a tall, dark haired man enter the ballroom and her heart gave a sharp jolt. Then she recognized the auburn hair of her niece and breathed a sigh. It was Sinjin. But her relief was short-lived, for a second later Victor appeared, along with Rory.

Dressed in black formal attire, the three Rayborne brothers together were downright staggering, and the men in the room all took notice, as well as every woman.

Victor wore his hair back in a queue, emphasizing his impressive bone structure. The past week had been an absolute blur, and she had said nothing to him about Selene, waiting for him to come out with the truth, but she could not wait another day.

"Well, they certainly know how to make an entrance, don't they?" Janet said, a devilish smile on her lips.

Loraine snorted, and Janet frowned.

Lillith had not said anything to Janet about what Loraine

had told her. She had not been able to share the news with anyone, as if doing so would make it true.

Victor's gaze scanned the ballroom, and when he saw her, he smiled. The breath lodged in her throat. She was tired of living a lie.

She had spent too many years being lied to, and she would not stand for it a moment longer.

Her attachment had been a palpable thing, waiting for him to come by, looking for him out the window, aching for his touch, for the next time he would fill her and bring her to completion again and again . . . and all along he had been seeing Selene, the mother of his unborn child.

A child that Lillith could never give him.

Lady Rochester would no doubt be bothered by the news at first, as she had not seemed very fond of Selene, but an heir to the Rayborne dynasty would be a welcome addition, indeed.

Victor was standing before her a moment later, his blue eyes sweeping her length, making her feel like the only woman in the room as his lips curved into a devilish smile she felt all the way to her toes.

She sincerely doubted there would ever be another man who would make her feel this way.

Loraine cleared her throat. "Well, Janet, let's give the two some time alone," she said, her voice clipped and curt.

Victor watched their retreat. "Was it something I said?" he asked, sounding amused and not at all concerned.

Lillith wondered if he felt guilty at all, or if a man like him did not let emotion play into it. How easy would it be to just go through the motions, take lovers at will and when it struck your fancy; babies and other women were a mere afterthought. She sighed inwardly, wishing not for the first time in her life that she had been born a man.

"You look lovely, Lily."

"Thank you," she murmured, the hair on her arms standing on end as he kissed her knuckles.

"So did you manage to tie up all the details for Marilyn's coming out?"

"Yes."

"If you have any questions, I'm sure my mother would be only too happy to assist you."

How ironic that not so very long ago she was at a party where he was to find a bride. Indeed, she doubted his parents had relinquished the pressure on him to marry.

It's not like he would have ever married her. No, Lord and Lady Rochester would never approve of an aging widow as a good choice for their son who had not seen his thirtieth year. Even an actress in her early-to-mid twenties would be preferable to a barren noblewoman.

"I do hope Marilyn finds someone suitable," Lily finally said, forcing a smile she did not feel. "She deserves nothing but the utmost happiness."

His eyes narrowed slightly. "What is wrong, Lily?"

Was she so very easy to read?

She glanced past him to Sinjin and Katelyn, who had stepped out onto the dance floor. How happy her niece was, her smile radiant and only for Sinjin.

"Nothing."

He took a step closer, and it was all she could do not to take a step back. "Tell me the truth."

They were far enough away from everyone else that no one could hear their conversation. She swallowed past the lump in her throat, weighing her choices. She could act as though nothing was wrong, but it would eat at her all night long. "I understand that you are to be a father."

His eyes never wavered from hers. He barely blinked, and for a moment she knew that Loraine had to have been misinformed. That is until Victor said, "I do not deny it."

Her heart crashed to her feet. To hear the accusation from her sister was one thing, but to hear the truth from his lips was altogether devastating. Visions of Victor and Selene in a heated embrace came to her, his naked body moving over the other woman, her nails clawing into his back as he thrust inside her over and over again, on their rented hotel bed . . . in the middle of the afternoon.

She felt constricted and locked her knees. By God she would not show him how the news affected her.

"Selene says the baby is mine and there is no way to know for sure, Lillith."

Her heart pounded so loud it was a roar in her ears. "But you could be the father."

"Yes."

"And did you meet her at The Grand Hotel this week?"

His eyes narrowed. "Yes."

"Why did you not tell me?"

He swallowed hard, and she could see the look of desperation on his face. "I couldn't find the right moment."

Why, because he'd been too busy making love to her while trying to come up with what to tell his parents about his ex-mistress who was pregnant with his child?

"Did you kiss her?"

"It's not like that."

She went to move from him, but he reached out, his fingers curling around her wrist, holding her tight. His eyes were intense, more so than she had ever seen them.

"I should have told you. I know that." He cursed beneath his breath and raked a hand through his hair. "I have tried very hard to come to grips with the truth myself, Lillith. It's not that

I wanted to hide anything from you. I just didn't know how to tell you."

"Selene has wanted to get you back from the moment she stepped foot in Claymoore Hall, and now she has done just that." Lillith shook her head. "I should have known it would end this way."

"What does that mean?" he asked, the nerve in his jaw jumping. Dear God, he actually looked concerned.

Lillith pressed her lips together and drew in a deep breath. "What we had was lovely, Victor. I shall never forget those days for as long as I live. You made me feel so special. You made me feel desired, something I had not felt for ages, and for that I shall always be grateful. Thank you."

He turned white beneath his tan. "You no longer wish to see me."

She stared at him, taking in every beautiful feature, remembering him as he was now. Her pulse skittered. Was that actually vulnerability she saw in his eyes, or merely a practiced expression that he perfected through the years? For all she knew, he would leave this ball relieved that it had all been so easy. Perhaps it had all been contrived for this particular outcome. Now he would be a husband and a father, just like that. No more barren widows to worry about.

With a thousand different emotions racing through her, she reached up and touched his cheek, her thumb brushing over his full bottom lip. "Good-bye, Victor."

18

Victor sat alone in the corner drinking black bitter coffee as he waited for one man's arrival. A couple of acquaintances had approached him but left him alone just as quickly, realizing he was in no mood for conversation.

He was on a mission tonight.

He had made a huge mistake, and now he had to rectify it. And he could not do that until he had the truth.

He no longer trusted Selene. Like Lillith had said, she had wanted him back from the moment she had come to Claymoore Hall, and he would not put a fake pregnancy past her.

It was a sick, desperate ploy to use, but people did very strange things when pushed.

The door opened and a gust of wind blew into the room, followed by the stout figure of Count de Lamonde. He removed his hat, coat, and gloves, and shoved them into the hands of the attendant before walking toward a table marked RESERVED. A wide smile lit the man's face, but that smile faded as his gaze shifted to Victor.

He squared his shoulders and lifted his chin.

Victor stood and walked toward the count who had yet to move an inch.

"I need a word with you."

The man's eyes narrowed into slits. "We have nothing to discuss."

"I think you'll want to hear what I have to say," Victor said, motioning toward a nearby table.

The count followed him to a table where they both sat down. A server approached, but Victor shook his head, so he nodded and walked away.

"What is this about?" the count asked, his French accent heavy, the words heated.

"Has Selene told you she is pregnant?"

The count's eyes widened, and he looked over each shoulder. "No, she has not."

"She has told me that she's pregnant and that I'm the father."

The count's hands clenched into fists until his knuckles turned white. "How far along is the pregnancy?"

"I'm assuming that it would be about three months."

He nodded, looking surprisingly calm. "And you have not been with her during that time?"

"No, I have not."

"How did you find out?"

"She told me herself."

The count took a deep breath, released it. "What else did she tell you?"

"Only that I am the father."

"Interesting." Howard sat back in the chair heavily and brushed a hand over his face. "Well, I can set your mind at ease, Lord Graston. Selene is lying."

"What makes you say that?"

"Not even a month ago she was menstruating. I remember because she was cramping especially bad."

Hope flared within Victor's chest. Selene had horrible cramps that left her bedridden for days. "You are sure."

Howard nodded, "Yes, I remember it clearly. I saw the soiled rags for myself. I had called for the maid to make a special compress for her stomach because she was in so much pain."

Victor breathed a sigh of relief.

"Do you intend to talk to Selene?" Howard asked, his gaze intense.

"If what you say is true, and I believe it is, then I have nothing to talk to her about." Victor extended his hand and the count took it. They shook hands, and without another word, Victor walked out the door, feeling like the weight of the world had been lifted off his shoulders.

Lillith passed by Thomas into the opulent three-story Georgian townhouse. He had been right. The property was exquisite and had been renovated in a way that showcased the original details.

The problem she was having was not with the property itself, but with the memory of the night at the hideaway. She couldn't get the sordid images from her thoughts: the infamous highwayman costume and Cleopatra, the bondage and all the events that happened thereafter. He hadn't said a word about that night, but then again, she would have been horrified if he had. They had instead pretended that it hadn't happened, and she was just fine with that.

Now if only she could forget.

He stood close, and she could feel the heat from his body. The cologne he wore surrounded her, and it was so overpowering it was hard to draw breath. She could tell by his behavior with her that he was interested in her sexually—the easy smile, the way he rested a hand on her hip as they walked up the staircase.

"Are you interested, Lillith?" he asked, his voice suggesting something other than an interest about the property. And he had called her Lillith, he'd not used her title. At least he had not called her Lily. Only Victor and his brothers had called her by her nickname and it would seem odd for another man to do so.

At any other time she might have jumped at a property such as this, but she was exhausted, both mentally and physically, and she could not stop thinking of Victor—of the way they had broken things off, of him with Selene, and if they were even now planning a wedding.

She was waiting for the banns to be posted any day now.

Lord help her, but she missed him. Most ardently. She had lain in bed for days and cried herself to sleep. It had been Janet who had pulled her out of bed and told her to snap out of it.

And her friend was right. It would get better with every day that passed, and she would survive, just as she always had. It was just as well she did not have Victor in her life any longer. The relationship would have only ended in grave disappointment.

"I like it very much," Lillith said, pulling herself back to the present. "If it is all right with you, I shall contact my solicitor and have him look at the property as well."

"Excellent," Thomas said. As they walked through the rest of the home, he highlighted the prominent features and she became even more enchanted with the property.

"Shall we have dinner afterward?" he asked, taking her by surprise.

"Oh, I do not know. It has been a long day."

He looked crestfallen. "Please, it is my treat."

Honestly, what did she have to lose? "Very well."

* * *

The restaurant was full to bursting, and they were seated at a table in the very center of the restaurant. She was aware of others watching them, and she was surprised how very little she was beginning to care what others thought of her. The blinders had been taken off so to speak, and she was finished with constantly worrying about other people's opinions.

"May I ask you a question, Lady Nordland?" he asked, boyish smile in place. He really was handsome, his blond curls glimmering under the light of the chandeliers, his brown eyes warm, his features pleasant.

"Of course you may," she said, steadying herself for what was to come.

He leaned forward, and she did as well. "Will you be attending the hideaway next week?"

She sat back. "No, I most certainly will not."

His brows lifted and he actually looked surprised. "You did not find it to your liking?"

"I can honestly say that I did not."

His eyes drifted to her lips. "Perhaps in time that could change."

"I am not comfortable in attending such a place. However, I do not begrudge those who do," which was the truth. She had learned that people must do what made them happy.

"I am sorry to hear that. I think you might have come to enjoy yourself."

"Perhaps," she said, doubting it very much. Desperate to change the subject she blurted, "So tell me, do you have any other properties you could show me?"

"Yes, I do," he said, all talk of the hideaway forgotten.

They ordered their meal and spent the next hour talking about real estate and the possibilities with the property he had just shown her. She was shocked when she looked up to find a familiar figure standing in the lobby watching her.

Selene. She looked stunned to see Lillith and Thomas together. Lillith turned her entire attention over to Thomas and didn't look in Selene's direction again until she walked toward her on the arm of an older gentleman.

Was this the infamous count who was so besotted with her? But why would she still be seeing the count if she was pregnant with Victor's child?

She mentally shook her head, telling herself she was a fool to be trying to figure out the tangled web of lies.

Lillith hadn't yet touched the Madeira Thomas had ordered for her, but now she lifted it to her lips and drank deeply. He grinned and took a drink from his glass.

The count slid a possessive hand around Selene's waist. The man was three times her age, short, with thin, graying hair, and a thick waist. The two were very oddly matched, and it didn't take a genius to figure out why the young beauty was with him.

Selene touched the emerald necklace that came to a point right above her ample décolletage. Matching earrings hung from her lobes.

Lillith felt an intense dislike for the other woman that bordered on disdain. Thomas must have seen her reaction, because he reached for Lillith's hand and brought her fingers to his lips and kissed her tenderly.

She knew he did so in order to make her feel better, and she was grateful he was trying to help her save face in front of her rival.

As the couple passed by and finally took a seat in a nearby corner, Lillith let her hand slide from his. "Thank you," she said with a smile.

He winked. "Anytime, Lillith. Anytime."

Victor was ready to rip someone's head off. Namely, Thomas Lehman's.

He had it on good authority that Lillith had been out to dinner with Thomas, and he was not happy about it. He told himself, the two could have been out discussing business and properties, but he had a feeling the other man had a plan, and being a man himself, he knew well what that plan entailed.

Apparently the flowers Victor had sent along with the note he'd attached had gone unnoticed and unacknowledged. He was unaccustomed to a woman being so . . . determined to stay away from him.

But he was a man who was used to having his way, and he knew what he wanted, and he wanted Lily.

Which is why he was on her doorstep, knocking at the door, hoping she wouldn't tell him to leave and never come back.

Perspiration broke out on his brow, and he felt nervous and unsettled. The sound of approaching footsteps made his heart accelerate.

Bloody hell, what was wrong with him? He knew women, knew what to say, how to charm them, how to get his way.

But perhaps he had met his match in Lillith.

The door opened and Edward, Lillith's valet, appeared. "My lord," he said, giving a curt nod. His expression gave away nothing.

"Hello, Edward. Will you please tell Lady Nordland that I am here?"

"I fear she is gone for the afternoon, my lord."

"Do you know where she has gone?"

He cleared his throat and did not even blink. "I shall tell her you came by, my lord."

Realizing further prompting would get him nowhere, he nodded. "Thank you, Edward."

The door closed, and he turned and walked down the steps. The boy who had worked at Lady Dante's and now worked for

Lily passed by him, up the steps. He smiled at Victor. "Good afternoon, my lord."

"Good afternoon, Zachary. Do you know where Lady Nordland might have gone to?"

"Yes, I was with the driver when we dropped her at Hyde Park."

Victor tipped his hat. "Thank you, lad."

Victor arrived at the park twenty minutes later. There was such a huge crowd it would be difficult to find Lillith, but he was determined. He walked endlessly, along each pathway. He did not realize how tough a task it would be. Nearly every woman wore a bonnet, and he had approached a blonde more than once, only to find it wasn't Lily.

He had removed his jacket and was seriously considering coming back on horseback when he heard her soft laughter ring out. Lily stood with Thomas and another man, who was close to her age and had a pencil-thin moustache and a monocle to his eye.

They were all laughing now. She had never looked more beautiful to him as she did with the sun shining down on her. The walking dress was made of cambric and was a pale lilac. She held a parasol, and she gave off a youthful vitality.

Thomas touched her elbow as he spoke to her, and she nodded, a pleased smile on her lips.

Victor's blood ran cold. Was he losing Lillith to the Irish rogue? Maybe she had turned to the other man in order to forget about him.

He walked toward the group in long strides. Thomas caught sight of him and alerted Lillith who turned, the smile disappearing before his eyes.

"Lord Graston," she said, not at all hiding her surprise at seeing him.

He bowed. "Lady Nordland, I dropped by your house to see you and I was told you were here."

She looked disappointed. Was she upset that he was here or that her staff had told him where to find her? "I see," she said, shifting on her feet.

He wondered if the flush in her cheeks was from the joy she felt at being with her companion or from the shock of seeing him. "You look well," she blurted.

"As do you, Lady Nordland," he said, taking her hand in his, kissing her fingers.

The pulse in her neck accelerated, and she licked her lips and promptly pulled her hand away. "So . . . what brings you here this afternoon?"

"I had to see you." The words were out before he could stop them.

The man with the monocle stood up straighter. "Is everything all right, Lillith?"

Victor glanced at him and the man's eyes narrowed.

"Would you give me a moment alone with Lord Graston, gentlemen?"

Thomas's expression was difficult to decipher, but he gave a nod, as did the man with the monocle.

Victor took Lillith by the hand and led her away, toward a bench beneath a towering oak tree. She sat down, then smoothed out her skirts. She was actually trembling.

"What is so important that you had to follow me here?"

"I miss you, Lily."

She closed her eyes, took a deep breath, and released it before opening her eyes once more. "You don't even know me, Victor, and it's apparent that I don't know you."

"Selene's not pregnant."

She opened her mouth and snapped it shut just as quickly.

A lock of hair had fallen free of her chignon. He reached up and touched the soft curl. He remembered how she looked with her hair down while they were making love. How different she had been in the privacy of the bedchamber. So different than the straight-backed lady he watched now.

She pushed his hand away. "How do you know?"

"I had a discussion with the count. Selene is not pregnant. In fact, she never was. She lied to trap me." He took her hands in his. "Forgive me, Lily, for putting you through this. I know it was not easy for you."

She looked down at where their hands were joined. "It was not easy, and that is why I am hesitant to see you again."

"I swear I will not hurt you again."

"You told me that before."

He nodded, "I know. If I could have saved you from this, I would have. Please give me another chance."

"You know for certain she is not with child?"

"Yes, the count set my mind at ease. He can deal with Selene now. I want nothing more to do with her."

Lillith pressed her lips together and looked past him to the two men. "I must go now. I have an appointment to show my solicitor a property I'm interested in buying."

"Will you meet me at my house later?"

Her gaze searched his and he knew she fought an inner battle. "I don't know."

By the time Lillith arrived at Victor's townhouse she was nervous and on edge. What a shock it had been to see him. One moment she was nursing her wounds, the next he was hunting her down to tell her that Selene was not pregnant. She was still elated by the news, and yet understandably wary.

She must be smart from here on out and guard her heart well.

Jeffries welcomed her at the door and led her toward a study where mahogany bookcases lined the walls. There was not a single space available for any new books, and Lillith wondered if the infamous Rakehells of Rochester had even read a single tome.

She walked over to a cupboard where crystal carafes held a variety of liquor. She reached up, grabbed a glass, and poured herself a small amount of scotch, then downed it in one swallow. Her eyes watered and she savored the burn as it worked its way to her stomach.

The door opened behind her and someone approached. Excitement raced along her spine. When she had seen Victor earlier today, her heart had skipped a beat. Lord how she had missed him, and as much as she told herself she was better off without him, she realized that getting over him would be difficult.

She set the glass down and before she could turn, he stepped up to her, his body heat radiating into her.

Victor.

He kissed the top of her head and she closed her eyes.

His lips were at the back of her neck, her shoulder. Her breath caught in her throat; her nipples stabbed against the bodice of her gown.

His large hands slid around her waist, upward, cupping her full breasts, his thumbs brushed over her sensitive nipples, teasing the peaks into tight buds.

His huge cock pressed hard against her back, just above the curve of her buttocks. He reached beneath her skirts, his hands moving up her thighs and straight to the slit in her drawers.

His fingers brushed over her clit. His lips pressed against the side of her neck and she breathed deeply, opened her eyes, and caught their reflection in the mirror above the fireplace. His dark head was bent, her breasts nearly out of her gown, and her nipples protruding above the low neckline. He lifted her in his arms a moment later and placed her on the settee, sliding between her thighs.

She looked toward the door, but he reached up. "It's locked," he said, drawing her attention back to him.

Her heart raced as he lay on her, his cock pressed firmly against her hot mound. He smoothed the hair off her face and kissed her softly.

Heat flooded her belly, slipping low to her groin. He was so handsome, and she had missed him so much.

She grabbed his buttocks and squeezed the firm cheeks. He cupped his hips, his cock like stone against her. She released a low-throated moan she hardly recognized as her own.

He took a nipple into his mouth and teased the bud with his tongue until she was moving beneath him, desperate to feel the length of his cock inside her weeping core.

She unbuttoned his trousers, then sighed as she took his cock in her hand, savoring the feel of satin over steel, and guided him to her entrance.

He smiled against her lips and slid inside her welcoming heat with a groan.

Lillith arched her hips, taking him in as deeply as possible. He kissed her softly, his tongue gliding over hers, matching the rhythm of his cock thrusting into her.

The stirrings began deep inside, and with each stroke, she drew nearer to orgasm. He pulled away the slightest bit and she opened her eyes. The desire in those brilliant blue depths took her breath away.

"Come with me, Lily," he said, his thrusts long and fluid. She watched his long length slide in and out of her.

He flexed his hips, putting pressure right on her tiny button, and she cried out as the first contractions began.

Lily's snug walls tightened around him as she met her climax.

She said his name on a moan and he smiled as he buried his face in her blond curls, thrilled to have her back. Her nails bit into his buttocks, urging him toward his own completion. Her fingertips brushed against his spine, up over his shoulders, down his arms, where she gripped his biceps.

She kissed his neck, her tongue teasing the lobe of his ear, swirling along the ridge.

He came with a loud groan, not caring if he woke his little brother who was still slumbering after a late night.

19

Rory glanced at the woman in his bed. They had spent the past few hours making love, and he knew something was off. Anna had been uncharacteristically quiet all evening. "What's wrong?" he asked, smoothing his hand over her slender back.

She looked at him, her dark eyes filled with sadness. "What do you think of me, Rory?"

It was an odd question, especially coming from Anna, who had always been confident.

"I think you are wonderful."

"I am not seeking your praise," she said with a sigh. "I want to know the truth, and you of all people should be honest with me. After all, you are my friend."

They were, indeed, friends, and he would help her in any way he could. "What do you want to know?"

She sat up a little, bringing the pillow beneath her breasts. "What do men think of me?"

He did not want to be having this particular conversation with her, for he feared she would not like the answer. She was an incredible lover, and most men of his acquaintance were not afraid to share stories about their liaisons with Anna. Unfortunately, because of her enthusiasm in the bedchamber, her reputation was blighted because of it. Most man seeking a wife would never consider Anna as a suitable bride, save for an old widower who didn't care about reputation, particularly those having lived through one arranged marriage.

"They speak highly of you . . . in the bedchamber."

She sighed and buried her face in the pillow.

He brushed a hand down her back, over the soft curve of her ass. "What is wrong? Why the sudden worry?"

She looked up at him. "Will you be attending the coming-out party for Lady Marilyn?"

"Of course."

"Do you think she will find a husband when it is all said and done?"

"Lady Marilyn is a lovely woman. I have every confidence her launch will be successful and that she will find a suitable mate."

She didn't say a word, just stared straight ahead.

"Why, are you worried she will draw a certain man's favor?"

She dropped her gaze to the sheet between them, her top teeth worrying her bottom lip. He had never seen her look so forlorn. "No."

"Then why so curious all of the sudden?"

Her dark eyes met his. "I think she is beautiful, that is all."

He knew the look in her eyes, recognized what it meant, what her questions meant. "Oh my God, you like her?"

She looked up and their gazes caught and held. "I consider her a friend."

"But you wish her to be more."

She didn't deny it. "Can you keep a secret?"

Intrigued, he nodded.

"Lady Marilyn's mother caught us in a rather compromising situation, and I don't think I'll ever be able to get to see her again. I was not even invited to the debutante ball."

"She is sister to my future sister-in-law, and I can certainly help in any way I can. Do you wish to attend the ball?"

"No, I would not dream of going, especially since Marilyn does not expect me there, but will you take her a message from me?"

"Of course."

Her lips curved into a smile. "Thank you, Rory." Her gaze shifted over his chest, drawing lower over his abdomen and lower still. "I'll make it up to you."

Rory entered the parlor of Lillith's townhouse and took a seat in a chair near the fire. He removed his damp gloves and held them up to the flames.

The valet had left him to his own devices after telling him that Marilyn would not be returning for at least an hour.

Rory had told him he would wait until Marilyn arrived. He was still surprised how solemn Anna had been when she'd talked to him about Marilyn. In all the time he had known her, she had never been so subdued, and he wondered at the extent of her feelings for Marilyn.

All the way over he had wondered if he was doing the right thing by Marilyn in telling her how Anna felt. After all, she was young and innocent—the exact opposite of Anna.

But Anna was his friend . . .

The door opened and he turned. A young maid entered with a silver tray. Her blond hair was worn in a loose bun at the back of her head, and she wore a simple gown and apron. "Tea, my lord?" she asked, not once making eye contact.

She was lovely, her lashes thick and long, her nose small, and her lips deliciously full, the top tilting up the slightest bit. His cock jerked against the buttons of his trousers.

"What is your name?"

"Shannon, my lord."

"Yes, I would love a cup, Shannon," he said, his voice coming out husky.

She set the tray down on a nearby table, turning her back to him. She was slender, perhaps too much so, and she had soft tendrils of long, silky hair falling from her haphazard coiffure. How he would love to kiss the nape of that neck, see her naked.

"Cream and sugar?" she asked, glancing back at him, making eye contact for the first time.

The breath left his lungs in a rush.

Her eyes were truly amazing, light blue and piercing. His gaze shifted over her fragile features to the delicious lips. He glanced at her small, firm breasts. Realizing where his attention had been diverted, he ripped his gaze back to her face, and a finely arched brow lifted as she waited for him to answer.

"Oh, yes," he said, recalling her question. He hoped he did not come across as a complete buffoon.

He did not drop his gaze as she poured the cream into the cup, then placed two lumps of sugar inside. "Would ye like more?" she asked, her voice unique, and he noted a hint of an Irish accent.

"No, thank you, Shannon."

She handed him the cup and he noticed she trembled. Was she nervous?

"Are you hungry, my lord?" The accent was mysteriously gone.

"Yes," he said, even though he wasn't hungry in the least. He wanted her to return, wanted her company and yearned to know all about her.

"The cook made scones just this morning. They are wonderful, especially with the fresh jam she made last week."

Everything about her intrigued him. "That would be delightful, Shannon. Thank you for your hospitality."

She smiled then, and the effect was devastating on his senses. She had small, straight white teeth,.

He watched her walk to the door and slip out of the room. He sat back in the chair and took a sip of tea. The blood in his veins simmered.

His mother had said not to dawdle with the help, but in this case, he might make an exception. Shannon was a beauty, flawless in every way.

The door opened and he set his cup down when Marilyn appeared.

"What a pleasant surprise," she said, removing her bonnet and tossing it on a table as she walked toward him.

"I am glad you think so," he said, kissing her cheek.

"Edward said you have been waiting awhile."

"I dropped by your mother's home, but she said I could find you here."

"Yes, I am to meet Lillith to discuss details about the upcoming ball. Tell me that you will be attending."

"I would not dream of missing it, Marilyn."

She grinned. "I am so glad."

He sat forward in his chair. "I am here because a mutual friend of ours wants to see you again."

Her lips curved into a coy smile. "Why did this friend not come himself? Is he too afraid of my mother?"

"Actually, *she* did not know if she would be welcomed."

The smile slid from her lips and she folded her hands in her lap. "Forgive me, but I find this all rather strange, given the fact you are Anna's lover."

The door opened and Shannon entered, keeping her gaze to the floor. She set the tray with a plate of scones, clotted cream, and jam next to him. "Will there be anything else?"

"Nothing for me, Shannon. Thank you for looking after me while Lady Marilyn arrived."

She nodded. "Lady Marilyn, can I get you anything?"

"I am fine, thank you, Shannon."

They waited until she was out the door.

"Yes, it is true Anna and I have an intimate relationship, but let me assure you that I feel no emotional attachment."

Marilyn winced. "That does not make it any better, Rory."

"It might be difficult to understand, but it works for us. I respect her and she respects me. She is my friend, Marilyn. Just take time to hear her out."

"My mother does not want her near me," Marilyn said, standing. She flattened a hand over her stomach. "I do not know when next our paths will cross."

"She's in my carriage as we speak."

Marilyn paled.

"Just go for a short ride around the park. She wants only to talk, Marilyn. That is all. A few minutes of your time is all I ask."

Marilyn walked to the window and looked down on the carriage below. She toyed with a lock of dark hair. "I will talk with her, but only for a few moments."

Rory smiled inwardly. "Thank you."

"What will you do?"

"I shall eat a scone, and perhaps another. They look delicious."

"If my aunt arrives, tell her that I forgot something at my mother's, will you?"

"Of course." He did not tell her he was not worried about Lily arriving since she was still at the townhouse when he had left. Her meeting with her niece might have slipped her mind.

Marilyn's heart pounded in time to her steps. The closer she came to the carriage, the more she yearned to run. And yet she had to get this over with. Just this morning a young baron had come calling at her mother's home, a brother of one of the other debutantes.

He was worth 2,000 pounds a year, and he seemed like a nice enough fellow. Unfortunately, he wasn't handsome; but he had a great personality and a witty sense of humor. Those were all good qualities in a husband.

The footman who had been standing beside the lamppost walked over and opened the carriage door.

Marilyn climbed into the dark interior and took the seat opposite Anna.

She wore a modest burgundy and gold daydress. A slender gold chain with a cameo hung from her neck, nestled between the creamy slopes of her breasts.

"You wished to see me?" Marilyn said, feeling her cheeks grow warm.

"I am sorry about our last encounter. I hope your mother was not too upset."

"She was furious."

Anna did not drop her dark gaze. "I do so wish I had heard her before she walked in."

"Perhaps it is for the best that she did see us."

Her brows furrowed. "Why do you say that?"

"Because it is the truth." Marilyn folded her hands in her lap.

"You do not mean it."

Marilyn did not even blink. "I do mean it . . . with all of my heart. We do not belong together."

Anna stared at her for a long moment, and before Marilyn could blink, the carriage started moving, and Anna slid into the seat beside her.

Marilyn could feel the heat from the other woman's body permeating through her dress, into her thigh. "Where are we going?"

"Just around the park. Do not fear, I am not kidnapping you."

"This is a mistake."

"No, it's not." Anna reached up and touched Marilyn's cheek. She did not have gloves on and her fingers were soft. Her touch heaven.

Her hot breath fanned Marilyn's face; then her lips were pressed against her own. Her tongue swept into her mouth, urging a response.

What on earth was she doing? Marilyn pulled away. "You are Rory's lover."

"Yes." At least she didn't deny it.

"What if I were another's lover?"

"I would be jealous," Anna said earnestly. "I'm already jealous of the man you will one day marry."

"I am already being courted."

She looked stricken, and oddly, Marilyn was glad. She wanted Anna to hurt with the same ferocity that hurt her every time she thought of Anna with Rory.

"Even if you marry, I want to see you," she said, brushing her thumb over Marilyn's lower lip.

As Marilyn looked into her eyes, she realized that this was all a game. Perhaps she wanted what she could not have. Just like all the men in her life. She grew bored the moment she had them; then she was off looking for the next best thing.

She tapped on the carriage, and it rolled to a stop. "What are you doing?" Anna asked.

The door opened and the footman appeared. "I'm getting out," Marilyn said, taking the man's hand.

"Do not be silly, Marilyn," Anna said, her voice full of exasperation. "We are too far from your aunt's home. I have to return there to pick up Rory as it is."

Marilyn knew she was being childish, but she didn't trust herself, and so she just kept on walking.

20

Lillith had never felt so content, or that all was so right with the world. She and Victor had spent the morning in bed and then walked to the park where he had taken her out onto the lake in a rented boat. As the wind ruffled his dark hair, she had watched him, the sun shining across his handsome face, his eyes sparkling as his fingers wrapped around her calf. No one could see them, and she smiled as he picked up the oar and started rowing toward the bank.

He was dressed more casually than normal, his shirt made of fine linen and his pants made of soft doeskin. Knee-high black boots finished the simple ensemble, which she found very much to her liking.

"Where are we going?" she asked, glancing at the basket and blanket setting beside him.

The sides of his mouth lifted. "It is a surprise."

He had gone to great lengths to keep their events a secret, and joy rushed through her. He was thoughtful in so many ways, and she had never been so happy. As the days flew by, she became more enamored with him, more in love with him, and that terrified her, and yet exhilarated her too.

When she'd been a young girl, she had fancied herself in love with her husband, but what she felt for Victor was different than what she had felt for Winfred.

She thought of Victor always, and even dreamt of him. Since the day they had made up, he had stayed each night with her, spent nearly every available moment with her, much to her friend's annoyance.

But Janet was happy for her, and her nieces were downright giddy.

Victor steered the boat onto the sandy beach and jumped out. He helped her out, grabbed the basket and blanket, and tied the boat's rope to a nearby tree.

He took her hand and led her back into the trees, down a well-worn narrow pathway.

There was a small clearing where the sun shone through the trees. He spread the blanket out and set the basket down. "Please sit," he urged.

Lillith sat down, then smiled as he took a bottle of wine from the basket, two glasses, and an assortment of breads, cheeses, and smoked meats.

It smelled delicious and her stomach gave a grumble, which made him laugh.

He poured the wine into the glasses, and he lifted his to her. "To you, Lillith. For making me so happy."

She could not help the smile that came to her lips, or the overwhelming sense of contentment that rushed through her. She never imagined she would be so happy and so at peace with the world, and it was all because of him.

An infamous rakehell.

She sipped the wine, and accepted the cheese and bread he

handed her. Birds sang in the trees overhead, the breeze teasing the long locks of his hair.

"I want to take you to Rochester . . . to meet my parents."

She barely had time to swallow. He wanted to take her home? "When?"

"As soon as you are able." He brushed a thread from his trousers. "I know you are busy with Marilyn's coming out, but perhaps we could go for a long weekend before her mother leaves for Greece?"

"Yes, I would like that . . . very much."

He smiled and her heart gave a sharp jolt. He wanted to take her home!

He reached up and cupped her jaw with his strong hand, his thumb brushing over her lips. "I cannot remember a time I have been so happy, Lily."

His words pleased her to no end. "Nor I."

He leaned in and kissed her. "I love you."

Her pulse leapt at the declaration, and she grinned, never so happy. "I love you too."

She set down her glass and wrapped her arms tight around him. With a moan, he eased her onto her back, his hard body pressed firmly against her. He used his knees to spread her thighs wide and slid between them, his cock teasing her sensitive flesh. He kissed her again, his lower body moving against her, making her hotter with each stroke.

He lifted her skirts, pulling them high. "You are naked beneath your gown, Lily," he whispered against her lips.

"Do you disapprove, my lord?"

He lifted a brow. "Quite the contrary."

He made her feel positively wanton, bringing out a side of her she wished to further explore. A side of herself that she was beginning to love.

She deserved this happiness, she told herself, and she would make it an absolute priority in her life. She would make Victor a priority in her life, and nothing and no one would get in her way.

He moved down her body, kissing a path from her chest, over her belly; then he lifted her skirts and disappeared beneath them.

She gasped and moaned as his tongue danced over her folds, teasing her clit, sucking and laving until she felt the familiar stirrings of climax rippling through her.

Being out in the open where anyone could come upon them made her strangely excited.

Victor felt her sex quiver against his mouth, tasted the rush of her cream as it slid over his tongue.

"Victor," she said, arching her hips against him.

"Yes, my love."

"I want you inside me."

He slid inside her heat with a satisfied groan.

Lillith hands moved beneath his shirt, over his hot skin, feeling the play of muscle and sinew under her fingers. With each thrust she grew wetter, closer to orgasm.

Victor heard the snap of a twig but didn't look up. He could not stop if he wanted to. Telling himself it was merely the wind, he thrust deeper, and Lillith's quim gripped him tight as a glove, pulsing around his cock and pulling from him a climax that left him breathless.

Katelyn watched from the second-storey window as Sinjin got out of the carriage and rushed up the steps.

Her heart hammered in her chest as she wondered how he would take the news.

She heard the maid greet him and then his footsteps as he walked up the steps.

Good Lord, she was nervous. She took a steadying breath as the door opened and closed, and Sinjin appeared. Her stomach tightened. Before the party at Claymoore Hall that had changed her life, she had never dreamt of such happiness, and she thanked her lucky stars every day that everything had turned out as it had. She still could not believe her good fortune.

He pulled her into his arms and kissed her. "How did you sleep last night?"

"Very well," she said, looking up into his handsome face. She could not believe this man would soon be her husband. "And you?"

"Excellent, though I was worried when I woke and received your note saying you wished to speak with me immediately." He put her at arm's length. "Need I be afraid?"

She swallowed hard and saw concern flash in his eyes. "I am pregnant, Sinjin," she blurted before she lost her nerve.

He watched her closely, as though he was not sure he had heard her correctly. But as the seconds ticked by, a slow smile spread across his lips, and all the fear she'd been feeling melted away.

With a hand on either side of her ribs, he lifted her gently and kissed her.

"You are happy?" she whispered against his lips.

"Very."

She was so relieved.

"We must marry immediately," he said, setting her back on her feet.

The wedding was set for five months out, but that would not do. She did not want to walk down the aisle large with child, and she was glad he felt likewise. "Will your mother be horribly disappointed?" She knew Lady Rochester had been intent on a December wedding.

"My mother will be delighted to be having a grandchild.

Trust me in this." He laughed, a wonderful sound that thrilled her. "We must go to Rochester and tell my parents the good news."

Lillith was a nervous wreck by the time the carriage pulled into Victor's family's home in Rochester. The beautiful Elizabethan manor made of red stone had a multitude of mullion windows and gothic archways. Light filled every room, and the elegant furnishings were stunning. Lady Rochester took great pride in the estate, which was obvious in how she pointed out every single detail.

She was strangely intimidated by Lord Rochester, even though he had been nothing but kind upon meeting her. He had a head full of gray hair and the same beautiful blue eyes as his sons. He was tall, broad shouldered, but appeared frail for his size, his face gaunt.

Lady Rochester had smiled tightly during the introductions, and Lillith wished she knew exactly what the other woman was thinking.

"And here is your room," Lady Rochester said, coming to a chamber at the end of the hallway on the second floor. The room was decorated in ice blue silks, pale yellow, and silver adornments. A white marble fireplace had cherubs playing the flute, violin, and lute, flanked by rose vines.

"It is lovely." Lillith walked into the room, crossing to the blue silk drapes hanging from fashionable rods.

A large painting of the ocean crashing upon the rocks monopolized a wall where beneath were two chairs and a table. The initials B.R. were clearly visible in the bottom right-hand corner of the canvas. "Is this your work?" Lillith asked, turning to Betsy.

She nodded, "Yes, it is."

"It's beautiful," Lillith said, meaning it. "I like the use of blues and greens to show the dimension of the water."

"Do you paint, Lady Nordland?" Betsy asked, and Lillith shook her head.

"I do not, but I collect paintings. You are most talented, Lady Rochester."

Betsy's eyes lit up, and Lillith knew she had done well.

"Shall we continue our tour?" Victor asked, and Betsy nodded.

Victor's room was on the opposite side of the house and on the third floor. The chamber was huge, as was the dark, masculine furniture that filled it. A thick, dark brown blanket covered the large four-poster bed, and the fireplace was made of mahogany, simple in design, but perfect for the room.

A gold-striped settee and two chairs sat nearby. The artwork had a definite Eastern influence to it, and she wondered if he had traveled extensively in his life. There was still so very much she did not know about him.

That night at dinner they were joined by Sinjin and Katelyn, much to everyone's surprise. Katelyn looked radiant, and Sinjin was excited as he kissed her hand and announced, "Katelyn and I are expecting a child."

Betsy's shrill scream filled the room, and the next instant she was up, rushing toward Katelyn, hugging her. Lillith met her niece's gaze over the other woman's shoulder and smiled, tears tightening her throat. Katelyn had never been so happy, and Lillith was elated for her. Sinjin adored her, and she was confident they would have a good life together.

"You must marry immediately," Betsy said, and Katelyn and Sinjin looked at each other with relief.

"I have notified a priest already, Mother," Sinjin said reassuringly. "Rory is on his way home as we speak, and Katelyn's mother and sister should be arriving by tomorrow afternoon."

The quiet weekend they had planned would not happen, but Lillith did not mind. She stood and walked to her niece and embraced her. "Congratulations to you both. I am so happy for you."

"As are we, Lillith," Sinjin said.

Katelyn hugged her tightly. "Thank you, Aunt Lily."

They spent the next hour talking about the future, potential baby names, and where they would live. Betsy seemed distraught that Katelyn wished to stay in London during the pregnancy, and several times tried to convince her that country living was for the best.

Lord Rochester silenced her by clearing his throat or giving a curt shake of his head. At those times Betsy promptly clamped her lips together and remained quiet . . . for all of two minutes.

After a glass of brandy, Lillith was tired and excused herself to her room. Victor said he would walk her to her chamber.

"Are you disappointed about the wedding?" he asked after they left the dining room.

"Not at all. I am pleased for Katelyn, and I know she is excited about the child. It is good they are getting married straightaway. Now they will no longer be apart. She misses Sinjin so very much when they are."

"Your sister's home will be much more quiet from here on out."

"Yes, I suppose it shall be . . . until Katelyn has the child. I would hope she would come to visit her often, and me as well, as I love babies."

"Perhaps soon you will have a child of your own," he said, his eyes dancing.

Her breath caught in her throat. She forced a smile she didn't feel. "Perhaps."

He stopped, his hand sliding around her wrist. "I have said something to upset you?"

"I do not know if I am able to have children, Victor." The words were out of her mouth before she could stop them.

His brows furrowed and her heart sank to her toes. This was not the time or the place she had wished to discuss such matters, but since he had come out with it, then she might as well be forthcoming. She never wanted it to be said that she had tricked him in any way. "I see."

"You are disappointed."

"No, Lillith, I am just surprised." She could see the concern in his eyes, though. He was no different than any other man. He wanted children.

He smiled softly to put her at ease and brushed his lips against hers.

He walked her to the chamber door. "I shall return as soon as I am able. My parents shall retire early and I wish to speak to them about an important matter."

She wondered if he was going to talk to them about her. Is that why he had brought her home, to ask her to marry him? Now that she had told him about her inability to have children, would he change his mind? She lay down on the bed, closed her eyes, and cried herself to sleep.

21

The wedding was held in the chapel on the Rochester property, and only family and servants were in attendance. The bride and groom had eyes only for each other, and as Katelyn and Sinjin were pronounced man and wife, applause filled the small dwelling where guests lingered on wooden benches.

Marilyn and Loraine had arrived just this morning, and as usual, Loraine showed little emotion throughout the ceremony. It had taken everything Lillith possessed to keep the tears from falling, for she was so happy for her niece.

Victor looked incredibly handsome in a black suit with an emerald green waistcoat. She recalled last night when he had come to her room and he had made love to her so gently, so tenderly that she had felt precious. She had not asked him about his discussion with his parents, feeling she had no right to meddle in his affairs.

He looked at her now and smiled.

Her happiness was not long lasting. Walking back to the manor from the chapel, Loraine said, "I must speak with you."

"Can it not wait until we return to London?"

Loraine released a heavy sigh. "I think not."

What on earth was so important that she had to talk with her now? "Very well, after we have cake we can go for a walk in the garden. How does that sound?"

Lillith pulled her shawl tight about her shoulders and hoped whatever she had to say did not involve Selene MacLeod.

"It is difficult for me to say what I must, my dearest Lillith," Loraine said, and Lillith steeled herself for what was to come. After all, her sister had been the bearer of bad news of late.

Loraine cleared her throat. "I have heard it on good authority that there has been a wager that involves you."

Lillith frowned. "A wager?" Surely she must be mistaken. "What kind of a wager?"

"Between Victor and Rory."

Lillith released the breath she had not realized she'd been holding. "What wager do you speak of?"

"A wager that revolves around you becoming Victor's mistress."

"That is ridiculous."

Loraine shrugged. "Choose to believe or not, but I know it is the truth."

"How do you know the truth?"

"I promised I would not tell, but my friend found out by way of Rory's lover, who confessed to the wager one night while he was extremely drunk. It involves a pocket watch that belonged to a relative."

Lillith tried to recall if Victor had a pocket watch. She could not believe Victor would do such a thing. And she was tired of lies, of rumors, and people trying to make her miserable. She would just ask Victor himself about such a wager.

"I do not believe it."

"Very well," Loraine said, her eyes telling Lillith that she already believed the rumor to be fact. "If Victor seduced you into becoming his mistress, then he would win the cherished pocket watch from Rory. Apparently, that has come to pass."

"I shall find out for myself," Lillith said, hiding any hurt behind a forced smile.

Sinjin and Katelyn drove off in the carriage, headed for an extended honeymoon at Claymoore Hall where they had first met, and then would travel to Paris and spend a month in a flat right in the heart of the city.

Loraine had decided against leaving Rochford and said she would leave in the morning, along with her sister. Apparently she felt Lillith might need a shoulder to cry on.

She had been invited down to dinner and had thought perhaps she would wait until after to talk to Victor, but she could not wait. Instead, she went to his room and knocked on the door.

He answered seconds later and smiled upon seeing her.

"May I come in?" she asked, and he nodded, motioning her in.

What would she do if she found out the wager was the truth?

He removed his shirt and she stared at his powerful body, the rippling muscle beneath olive skin, and the broad shoulders where marks from her nails were still visible. She had not meant to be so aggressive, and her cheeks turned hot at the memory of making love in the park in the middle of the afternoon.

He pulled a shirt from his wardrobe and slid it on over his head. His dark hair appeared a moment later. He unbuttoned his trousers and her throat went dry. She quickly looked away, focusing on why she had come to his room to begin with.

"It was a lovely service, was it not?" she said, and he met her gaze in the mirror.

"Yes, indeed. I have never seen my brother so happy," he

said, tying his cravat with quick precision. Apparently he did not always rely upon a valet to help dress him.

Her gaze was drawn to his dresser, the polished top, the nearby cherry wood box, and the gold pocket watch sitting nearby. Her insides knotted. "What a lovely watch," she said, walking toward the dresser.

He said nothing, but she felt his gaze on her as she picked up the watch. "It looks like an antique."

"It is," he said, and something in his voice made her look up at him.

Was that fear she saw in his eyes?

"It belonged to my grandfather."

It involves a pocket watch that belonged to a relative.

She nodded. "It's lovely. Would you wear it tonight?"

"Of course."

He escorted her down to dinner, and she tried her best to keep her spirits up, but it was difficult.

Loraine sat opposite Lillith, her gaze shifting between her and Victor all night to the point Lillith finally nudged her shin. Her sister's brows lifted and she cleared her throat.

"Do you have the time, Lord Graston?" she asked, and Lillith's eyes widened at her sister's gall.

"Yes," he said, lifting the watch from his pocket.

"What a handsome watch," Loraine said, her gaze shifting to Lillith.

Lady Rochester glanced at her son. "Was that watch not given to Rory by your grandfather?"

Rory cleared his throat. "It was, but I gave it to Victor."

Loraine's lips curved into a triumphant smile, and Lillith felt her heart sinking to her stomach. Victor did not care for her. He had merely wanted to win a wager. A pocket watch at that.

Her cheeks burned and she nearly excused herself but forced herself to stay put.

"I am sure your brother will take good care of it," Lady Rochester said.

Victor reached for Lillith's hand and she jumped as though she'd been burned. She felt silly as others at the table looked at her oddly.

"Are you all right, Lady Nordland?" Lord Rochester asked, looking genuinely concerned, and Lillith nodded.

"Yes, my lord. I—um, felt a chill, that is all."

She could feel Victor's gaze on her.

"Lady Rochester, what a lovely portrait that is of you," Loraine said, pointing toward the painting over the sideboard. Lillith could have hugged her sister for drawing the attention away from her.

"It was painted many years ago, when I was far younger," Lady Rochester said wistfully.

"I can certainly see why Lord Rochester was smitten," Loraine said, pouring on the charm.

Lady Rochester's laughter filled the room, and Rory winked at Loraine.

"Lady Marilyn, I understand your coming-out ball is upon us. Are you excited?" Lady Rochester asked.

"I am, Lady Rochester," Marilyn said, doing her best to push her food around her plate. She knew her niece did not care for duck. Indeed, her appetite had been waning lately, and Lillith wondered if perhaps it was because of the upcoming ball.

Dinner dragged on for another hour, and it was great relief when finally Lord and Lady Rochester excused themselves and left the table, leaving just herself, Victor, Loraine, Marilyn, and Rory. She did not wish to discuss a delicate matter in front of the others, but Lillith could not keep her thoughts to herself another instant. "Did you make a wager about me?" she asked Victor, and across the table Rory, who had been talking to Loraine and Marilyn, went silent.

Victor closed his eyes and took a deep breath.

Her gaze shifted to Rory. "Did you make a wager with Victor involving the pocket watch?"

Rory glanced at Victor, who wiped his mouth with the napkin before tossing it on his empty plate.

"Yes, a wager was made, Lillith," Victor said, and the slight thread of hope she had held on to snapped.

Trembling, she stood and folded her hands together. "I fear I have made a huge error in judgment."

"Lily," Victor said, grabbing her hand, but she jerked away.

"I would ask that you leave me alone from this moment on. I no longer wish to be associated with you."

Loraine remained quiet, and Rory cursed under his breath.

Without another word, she rushed from the room.

Victor stood outside Lillith's room. She had locked him out and refused to answer the door. He could hear her inside, no doubt packing up her things, ready to leave as fast as she could. Her sister had not said a word to him, and Rory looked guilty as hell.

At least he knew whom to blame for opening his mouth.

Damn it!

The wager regarding the pocket watch had not entered his mind since he'd made it. In fact, he had been surprised to see the heirloom on his dresser soon after Rory's arrival.

Rory would never betray him that way, but he could have mentioned something in a moment of weakness.

And his brother had a weakness for women and liquor; a deadly combination if ever there was one.

He knocked on the door again.

Victor could take his chances and climb along the ledge of the window, but he was not even sure if she had kept the window open. Plus, given his luck, he would fall and break his neck. No doubt Lillith would be happy if that were the case.

"May I be of assistance, my lord?" Jeffries asked, producing a key from his jacket pocket.

He placed it in his hand and Victor smiled. "You are a godsend, my friend."

"I am glad you think so, my lord," he said, with a firm nod and a small smile before leaving him to it.

Victor unlocked the door and opened it. Lillith stood before the fire, staring into the flames. She did not even turn at his approach.

"Go away."

He flinched. "Lily, let me explain."

"What is there to explain?" She sounded weary.

"It was a friendly bet amongst brothers."

"What kind of man makes such a wager?"

He closed his eyes and counted to ten. "Point taken."

"I am exhausted, Victor. I thought that I had met a man who wanted me in the same way I wanted him."

"And I do want you. I love you," he said, stepping closer to her. He reached out to touch her, but she jerked away.

"You don't know what you want, Victor. You are still so young in so many ways. You do not care about anyone else's emotions, or how much your actions might hurt. I am too old to worry about such things."

"You are not old."

She shook her head. "I am tired. Please leave me alone."

"Marry me, Lily."

Her eyes widened. "You cannot be serious."

She may as well have slapped him. "I am serious. I want to marry you. I went to my parents last night and asked their permission. They have given me their consent."

"I have no wish to be any man's wife," she said with firm resolve. "I already lived through one marriage, remember?"

"Yes, I know, but it does not always have to be that way."

"I never trusted my husband, and I am finding it very hard to trust you. About the time I think I know you, I realize how very wrong I am." The words were said with a firm formality that made his blood run cold.

"Please go, Victor, let me be."

All of London was abuzz with the news.

Lady Nordland had been making love in a city park in the middle of the afternoon with an infamous rakehell. It was the "scandal of the season."

The person, who the newspaper referred to as "anonymous," stumbled upon the couple while hiking through a familiar path.

When asked by the reporter how he knew it was Lady Nordland and Lord Graston, said source had apparently waited in the trees and seen the two for himself, leaving their rendezvous with wide smiles and eyes only for each other.

Lillith was horrified. She had lived for nearly forty years safe-guarding her good reputation, and now she had thrown all caution to the wind and had been publicly humiliated.

What next, would they discover she had been to the scandalous hideaway?

Janet poured her another drink and handed it to Lillith. "All will be fine. You just wait and see. Soon another story will take its place and all will be forgotten."

Lillith appreciated her friend's attempts to make her feel better, but it was no use. She had made a horrible mistake and now she was paying for it dearly by way of public humiliation and a broken heart . . . and on the evening of Marilyn's coming-out ball.

"I am waiting for the message to arrive telling me that Marilyn is no longer invited to join the other debutantes. She will suffer because of my stupidity," Lillith said absently.

"Nonsense, mark my words in a few days' time, the scandal will blow over and none will be the wiser."

There was not a chance of the scandal blowing over any time soon. She knew society all too well, and that once a fallen woman, always a fallen woman.

At least Katelyn was married now, but poor Marilyn. Lillith would never forgive herself if she had ruined her niece's chances of marrying.

She could not show her face. Indeed, perhaps she should pack up her house and head to Bath? Come to think of it, Bath was not far enough away that scandal would not follow her there. Perhaps she would travel to Wales, to the seaside town her grandmother had taken them to during the summer.

"Come stay with me for a while, Lily," Janet said. "Get away from here, or I am happy to go anywhere you desire. I am at your disposal."

The words warmed her, and she knew Janet would go anywhere Lillith wanted. But she had no desire to leave her home. After all, this was her sanctuary. She would stay put. "No, I will not run."

A smile teased Janet's lips. "I believe in a few days' time that you will find you are quite popular."

Lillith frowned. "I sincerely doubt that."

"People love a scandal, especially women, and there is not a woman, married or unmarried, who is not envying you at this moment for the sole fact you had sex with Victor Rayborne, and in a public place."

"There was no one about, I assure you."

"Save for the 'anonymous source,' " Janet said with a shrug. "I am the last person to judge you."

The pain of having left Victor was still fresh in her mind. He had finally walked out of her chamber last night after apologizing and she had left his parents estate before first light.

Lord help her, but she already missed him, and a part of her was terrified she'd never see him again. She wondered how he was dealing with the rumor. No doubt it would only add to his reputation in a positive way, especially since she he was a renowned rakehell, where she would be ruined.

Life was so unfair.

"I have a delightful tea at my home that will calm you and help you sleep."

Lillith glanced at Janet. "Let me guess . . . it is laced with laudanum?"

"Of course not," Janet replied with a sheepish smile. "It won't take me but half an hour to make the round-trip."

No matter how tempted she was, she would not drug herself. "No, thank you." Instead, she would use this time to catch up on her reading and focus on what was important in life. Hopefully the charities she represented would not be distancing themselves from her. They had been such a large part of her life, after all.

"Well, I will return home, then, and let you get some rest, my dear." Janet kissed Lillith's cheek. "Are you sure you will not consider staying with me?"

"Thank you, but no." Lillith smiled. "You are a good friend, Janet."

Janet's lips curved. "As are you. I shall drop by tomorrow."

Lillith watched her friend leave, then fell into a chair. She tried to read, but found she could not settle her mind to save her life. To her dismay, her mind kept returning to the moment she had met Victor at Claymoore Hall, when he had flirted with her so outrageously, and the night they had first made love. She could barely remember the cold, frigid woman she had been before he'd come into her life. God, had it been only weeks?

Someone knocked at the door, and she was shocked to see that the sun was going down. How long had she been sitting here staring into the fire?

"Lillith."

Her stomach twisted as she looked up at the youngest Rayborne brother.

"I hope you don't mind that I let myself in?"

"No, not at all."

"Lily," Rory began, looking toward the chair beside her. "May I?"

She nodded, a thousand different emotions rushing through her at seeing him. He and his brother shared so many characteristics that it was difficult to look at him.

"I wanted to explain about the watch. It was completely my idea. Victor did not want anything to do with the wager, but I pushed him."

"He is a grown man, Rory."

"Yes, but it was my idea," he said, his fingers playing with the rim of his hat. "He had nothing to do with it, I swear."

"Did he ask you to come?"

Rory shook his head. "He has no idea that I'm here. Needless to say he wasn't happy with me after you left Rochester. It was I who opened my mouth to the wrong person. Too much liquor, I suppose," he said with a wistful smile. "I wanted you to know that he loves you very much, Lillith. He has never brought a woman home to Rochester to meet our parents."

Her heart missed a beat. She was stunned she had been the first, and even more stunned that they had given their consent for him to marry her.

"I am sorry, Lillith. Truly."

"I accept your apology, Rory, and thank you for coming."

He hesitated, as though he wished to say something else, but then he stood, and with a nod left her alone in the parlor with her thoughts.

22

Victor dropped back his second whiskey in as many minutes. He was back in London, and the city was alive with rumors about him and Lillith.

What kind of a man sold his story to the paper? If he could get his hands on the source, he would throttle him with his bare hands.

Lillith must be horrified that her greatest fear was coming to fruition. And it was all because of him. Why couldn't he have kept his hands to himself and just waited to make love to her back at his townhouse? He would never forgive himself for this, especially if she was ruined.

He chewed on his thumbnail and looked down on the wet streets. Rory had just exited the carriage and he took the steps two at a time. He rushed inside but stopped short when he saw Victor.

"I didn't realize you were coming to London."

"Why would I stay in Rochester and listen to Mother?"

"Point taken," he said, moving to the crystal decanter half full of Scotch. He poured a liberal amount into a glass and downed it in a single swallow.

Rory straightened, meeting his gaze head-on. "I went to see her."

He was still angry with Rory for opening his mouth about the wager. It was embarrassing to all involved. "Who did you go to see?"

"Lily."

He was not entirely shocked by the admission. He had gone out of his way to beg forgiveness at every turn, and Victor had accepted his apology more than once, but he had given him a warning to watch his mouth from here on out. After all, if one could not trust family, who could one trust?

"And what did she say?"

"That she forgave me. I told her that it was all my fault, and that you had nothing to do with the wager."

"But I did, Rory. I agreed to it, even when I shouldn't have, and she knows it." Victor brushed a hand through his hair. "I asked her to marry me, Rory, and she said no."

Rory's brows lifted. "Only because she's angry."

"Do you think so?"

"Of course. She loves you. Anyone can see that." He filled his glass again. "If you want to marry her, then go to her. Ask her again."

"She will say no."

Rory shrugged. "Then keep asking until she says yes."

Marilyn tried her best to relax, but it was nearly impossible. Stanley, Lord Ashcombe, had called upon her at her mother's home, and now they sat in silence in her mother's small study. They had talked about everything from the weather to her sister's wedding, but one topic had remained off-limits.

She had a feeling what was to come. After all, for the past few days all of London had been abuzz with the news. Her mother, in her exaggerated fashion, had been furious with Aunt

Lillith about her "impropriety," as though she herself wasn't sleeping with a much younger man. The only difference in the two situations was that Lillith had been caught making love outdoors and Loraine hadn't.

Poor Aunt Lillith.

Stanley paced the room. His large brown eyes were full of concern, his face uncommonly pale. He was a good man who would give her a good life . . . if she ended up marrying him. But was that even possible now?

"I wondered how you were faring," he said, pulling a kerchief from his pocket and wiping at his brow. "I was concerned."

"I am just fine."

"And your aunt?"

"She is well. Thank you for asking."

He nodded and shoved the kerchief back into his pocket.

She had never seen him so nervous. "Please sit."

He did as she asked, and he finally met her gaze. "Lady Marilyn, my parents have suggested that the ball be postponed until a later date—after the latest scandal blows over."

Marilyn shifted in her chair. "There is no need to postpone the ball on my account."

"What do you mean?"

"If they are embarrassed about me or my family, then I would not want to be there anyway."

"They do not have a problem with you," he said, his cheeks turning pink. "They just do not want the latest scandal casting a negative light on my sister and the other women's coming-out celebration.

"If they have a problem with my aunt, then they have a problem with me." She stood and walked toward the door, the feelings of inadequacy she had felt upon learning about her parentage brimming to the surface. Her own father had not wanted her and she had found out why—because she was not his daughter, but a servant's child. And now she felt like she was not quite good enough for Stanley or his family, and it infuriated her.

"Lady Marilyn, please do not be hasty."

"Your parents obviously do not approve of me, so there is nothing left to say."

He grabbed her hands and squeezed them tightly. "Marilyn, please do not make a rash judgment."

"It is you who are judging me, Stanley."

Perhaps this is what she had wanted all along. She had jumped at the chance to be courted by a baron when she had not even given herself a chance at any other man. She had just felt grateful for his attention and had liked the way it kept her from thinking about Anna.

"I swear to you that I am not judging you." He was desperate, she could see it in his dark eyes as he pleaded with her to understand.

And what she hated was that women had so little choice in life. She could not live on her aunt's charity forever, and her mother had made it clear she wanted her to marry. Yes, she could always live with Katelyn and Sinjin, because they had offered more times than she could count, but now with the baby on the way, she would not consider such a thing.

"Kiss me," she blurted.

He frowned and glanced at the door. "Your mother."

"Will not enter."

With a firm nod, he leaned in, licking his lips.

He had nice lips, she decided, and they were soft against hers, gentle even.

He was not that old, only four and twenty. She wondered how many lovers he'd had. As many as Anna perhaps?

Her arms slid around his shoulders, the muscle flexing. She

leaned against him, the sensation so odd compared to the times she had embraced Anna. Her body was so soft where his was so hard.

Knowing he would never deepen the kiss for fear of being improper, she took the initiative and teased the seam of his lips. To her surprise, he opened to her, his tongue sweeping into her mouth.

A delicious shiver rushed up her spine, making the blood in her veins turn hot. Her nipples hardened and pressed against her bodice. She wondered if he could feel her body's response, just as she could feel the hard ridge of his sex against the juncture of her thighs. What would his cock feel like? Would he be shocked if she touched him there?

The temperature in the room grew warmer by the second. Her hand moved to his hard abdomen, the muscles beneath her hand clenching.

Her heart rate accelerated when she heard Stanley's moan, felt his hips rock against her.

His hand braced the back of her neck, while his other hand slid to her wrist, guiding her hand to his manhood.

She felt him through the material of his trousers. He was so hard, and she ached to feel skin against skin.

He didn't move, and she wondered if he wanted her to stop. She had her answer seconds later when his fingers curled around hers and showed her the stroke he desired.

He grew thicker and longer in her hand, and his breathing rougher. He ended the kiss, his eyes dark as he stared at her, heavy lidded.

His hand slid from her neck, down her throat, to her breast. He cupped her, his thumb brushing over a nipple. She bit her lip against the delicious sensations rushing through her.

Abruptly, he stilled her hand, and his chest rose and fell heavily. He looked at her for a long moment and she wished she could read his mind.

She heard a chair scrape out in the hallway and abruptly pulled her hand away from him. He trembled as he righted his shirt and straightened his waistcoat and jacket.

Sweat gleamed on his brow and upper lip. "I would like to take to you dinner this evening," he said, his voice husky.

"I should like that very much," she replied, an excitement she had no idea she would ever feel again rushing through her.

"And I shall tell my mother that you will be attending the ball as intended."

Victor's gaze scanned the ballroom for the woman he loved. It had been an agonizing week since the scandal had broken, and thank God another had taken its place. That didn't mean anyone had forgotten about him and Lillith. The sly smiles from the men and women he passed by let him know that well enough, but he was past caring.

He wanted Lillith back and he wasn't going to leave here without her.

She sat in the corner beside Marilyn and a stocky young man who had not left the young woman's side all night.

Lillith smiled at something her niece said and Victor's heart gave a sharp tug.

Even from the distance he could tell she had lost weight. "Go get her, man," Rory said, clapping him on the back. His little brother had been his constant companion since their arrival back in London. Each night he had stayed in with Victor, and each day he tried to convince him to visit Lillith; but Victor had refused, hoping that perhaps with time he would get over her. After all, she had not accepted his marriage proposal. She had not even appeared interested. And what had she said about having been married before and not intending to again?

But time had only made him that much more aware of how

much he loved Lillith, how much he needed her in his life, and what lengths he would go to in order to have her.

A slender hand stopped him and he turned to find Selene smiling up at him. Her gown was scandalously low, and she wore, of all things, a diamond necklace and earrings he had bought for her on her last birthday.

Sinjin was right. He had been a little too generous with his lovers.

What the hell was she doing here?

"Did you not receive my letters?"

He had received them. "I did, and considering your lies, I thought it best to burn them . . . unread."

"I lost the baby."

"You are such a liar," he said, glancing past her, toward the couples on the dance floor.

Her brows furrowed and her gaze shifted slowly over him. "Meet me in the parlor just beyond the double doors. Please," she said, brushing her breast against his arm as she walked off, toward the double doors.

He was not at all enticed.

"Do not worry, brother, I shall take care of her for you," Rory said with a roguish grin that made Victor laugh.

He had little doubt his brother would do just that as he followed after Selene.

He turned his attention to Lillith. She knew he was here, and had been watching him and Selene until he'd looked at her. Now she spoke to Marilyn and her attentive beau.

As he approached, the young man stood and extended his arm to Marilyn. Marilyn flashed an encouraging smile as she passed by.

"Lily," Victor said, sitting down beside her.

He could feel the tension in the room, knew others watched

their every movement. Cheeks that had been pale suddenly bloomed with color.

"Lord Graston," she said, meeting his gaze.

Dark circles bracketed her eyes, making them appear more green.

"I've missed you, Lily."

She studied his face closely. Did she not believe him?

"What do you say we leave and go somewhere we can be alone?"

"I am chaperoning my niece, Victor. I am fortunate to even be here given the scandal."

"Do you care what these people think of you?"

"No, but I care what they think about Marilyn. She is my main priority."

He reached up and lifted her chin with gentle fingers. "Will you always put everyone else's happiness above your own? Come with me," he said, taking her hand and leading her outside onto the verandah.

He shut the door behind them and took the ring from his waistcoat pocket. He went down on his knee, then took her hand in his. "Marry me, Lily. Marry me and make me the happiest man in the world."

Tears shone in her eyes and he thought for a moment she would tell him no, when she nodded. "Yes, I shall marry you, Victor," she said, going into his arms. He held her close, savoring the feel of her against him.

"I will never make you question my love or my loyalty, Lily."

She smiled and pressed her cheek against his chest. "I love you, Victor. I cannot wait to spend the rest of my life with you."

The words he had been waiting to hear were like music to his ears, and he held her tight, not ever wanting to let go.

* * *

Rory entered the room.

Selene rested a hip against the settee, and seeing him, she stood up straight and frowned. "Where is Victor?" she asked, looking to the door as though he would magically appear.

"He is busy."

"With Lady Nordland?" she asked, her eyes full of jealousy.

"Perhaps."

She licked her lips. "Did he send you with a message?"

Rory shrugged and locked the door behind him.

Her brows rose to her hairline as he walked toward her.

He removed his jacket, then flung it over the back of a chair.

Her throat convulsed as she swallowed, and he could see the pulse at her throat quicken the closer he came.

Her gaze shifted over him, slowly down his chest, coming to an abrupt stop at his cock. He hadn't had sex for nearly a week, and he was more than ready. She licked her lips, her dark eyes not at all hiding her excitement as her gaze met his once more.

"The door is locked?" she asked as he leaned in for a kiss.

"Yes," he whispered, and at the last second he kissed the hollow of her neck.

She released a moan and reached for his cock.

He lifted her skirts, feeling the thigh-high stockings, the bare bottom.

"Lovely," he whispered, sliding his fingers over her hot slit. She cupped her hips against him as she fisted him in her hand, stroking him vigorously.

Two fingers entered her soaking entrance, and he easily added another. She cried out as his thumb brushed over her swollen clitoris, teasing it relentlessly.

Her channel gripped his fingers as she came, her fingers tightening on his cock as she rocked against him.

He turned her around, bent her over the edge of the settee,

and flipped her skirts over her back. Her plump buttocks were high in the air, and he slapped her ass until the white cheeks turned bright red.

Her fingers dug into the settee and she let out a whimper as he rubbed his cock against her, teasing her.

He played with her nipples, drawing them into tight little buds, pinching them as his cock nudged her weeping pot.

"Fuck me now," she cried out, and he slid inside her. She released a low-throated moan and arched her back.

He kicked her legs farther apart and smiled when her fingers worked her clit. Her inner muscles pulled him in deeper, and soon she was slamming back against him. He didn't even have to move.

Normally he was a generous lover, always making sure to bring the woman to completion first, but in this case, he did not bother. Let her leave wanting. She deserved it after everything she'd put Victor through.

He gripped her hips tightly and pumped into her with long, steady strokes.

She was getting closer to orgasm. He tweaked her nipples and she cried out, her fingers working harder; then with a final thrust, he pulled out and came on her back and upper buttocks.

She let out a discouraged moan, her fingers still working her clit, even as he cleaned off his cock with the hem of his shirt and slid it back into his trousers.

He walked toward the door, and he heard her finally find her release, her soft cries telling him she was more frustrated than excited. "You could learn a thing or two from your brother," she said, exasperation in her voice.

With a smile, he unlocked the door and ignored her when she told him to come back.

23

The carriage pulled to a stop in front of the beautiful Georgian manor that sat on the banks of the River Thames in Twickenham. The large estate stood behind a wrought-iron fence and came with a few acres of land, parklike grass, and a garden with every color of bloom imaginable.

"What is this?" Lillith asked her husband.

Husband.

She could still not believe she was married to Victor Rayborne, Lord Graston, and that they no longer needed to live apart.

The wedding had taken place within a few weeks of the banns, because Victor desperately wanted his father, who was quickly ailing, to be present.

Lillith had been stunned by how ill Lord Rochester had become in such a short period of time. But he had been all smiles at the wedding that had taken place at the chapel on the family's estate in Rochester, as had Lady Rochester, who told Lillith that she had never seen her son so happy.

It had been a trying couple of months, but Lillith wouldn't

change a moment of it for anything. She had learned that some things were worth fighting for, and that others would think what they wanted of you. It was beyond a person's control what others thought, and why waste time or energy concerning yourself with what you could not change.

A hard-earned wisdom that she would pass on to her nieces and their children.

All she knew was that she never wanted to be separated from the man she loved ever again.

Victor flashed a wolfish smile that made her heart beat in double-time.

"This, dear wife, is our new home."

"New home," she said, releasing a breath.

"That first night we went out to dinner you said that you wished you had a home on the river. Something close to London but with enough land that you need not worry that your neighbors knew your every move."

He had listened, and in turn bought her a home she would have never bought on her own. The home of her dreams. The *life* of her dreams.

"It is beautiful, Victor. I love it."

"I'm glad, my dear. I think we shall have many happy memories here." He opened the door and the footman helped Lillith down. Victor took her hand, and they opened the gate and approached the house where her servants were lined up on either side with Edward at the helm.

She would not miss the townhouse in London. She'd had too many memories of Winfred there anyway. Perhaps she could give it to Marilyn as a wedding present . . . whenever that time came.

They walked up the steps and before they entered, Victor lifted her high in his arms. She buried her face in his neck, but not before she saw the pleased smiles of her servants looking back at her.

A black-and-white marble entry greeted her, directly above a beautiful chandelier, the crystal stirring in the light breeze, filling the foyer with a pleasant tune.

The staircase split in two, leading up to the next floor.

Victor started for the one on the right.

"Are you going to carry me throughout a tour? You might become tired."

"We can take a tour later, madam. Now I have need to make love to my wife."

A few chuckles could be heard from the servants who still stood outside, and Lillith shook her head. Truth be told, she was just as anxious to find their bedchamber and make their union official as he was.

Their bedchamber was on the third floor and had an incredible view of the Thames. Victor set her on her feet, and she leaned back against him, his arms enfolding her. She laced her fingers through his.

Never had she imagined such happiness for herself.

"What are you thinking?" he asked, and she looked up at him, her heart squeezing with love for him.

"How very happy I am. How I never thought I would be here, with you." Indeed, she had imagined him settling down with one of the young debutantes his mother had brought to Claymoore Hall. Instead, he had chosen Lillith.

"I vow to always strive to make you happy."

"And I vow to do the same. I do not want any misunderstandings to come between us ever again. I want us to never go to bed angry."

He leaned down and kissed her gently, his lips firm.

"I love you."

"I love you, Lady Graston."

Lady Graston. The title still sounded odd to her, and oh so wonderful. Her old life was slipping away and she could not be happier.

They kissed, and he urged her into the room, until her back came up against the mattress.

"Wicked man," she whispered against his lips, and he grinned.

She felt that smile all the way to her toes.

Taking the initiative, she sat back on the bed. "Undress for me."

His brows lifted and he instantly began untying his cravat. Next, he shrugged out of his jacket and then unbuttoned his waistcoat and dropped it on the growing pile of clothing.

He removed his shirt, and her gaze shifted to the muscles of his abdomen that formed a V, leading to his beautiful cock. She could not keep the grin from her lips as he made quick work of his boots; then his hands moved to the buttons of his trousers.

Her mouth went dry as he watched her without blinking, his striking blue eyes turning darker as he slowly unfastened each button, then slid the pants down.

"Your turn."

She began with her hair, letting it down; then taking her time, she made a game of removing each piece of clothing until she stood before him in nothing but her stockings, high-heeled boots, and a smile.

His cock jutted from the nest of dark hair, rearing toward his flat belly.

His gaze moved down her body and back up again, stopping at the juncture of her thighs. "Lie down, Lily."

She climbed onto the bed and watched with anticipation as Victor walked toward the dresser where he produced what appeared to be a black silk scarf. Make that five silk scarves.

A sudden flash of memory came to her with Thomas at the hideaway.

"Victor, what are you about?" she asked, excitement licking her spine.

He tried to look innocent but failed. He tied each limb to the posts of the bed, leaving plenty of play for her to move. Just like the Cleopatra, she lay on her stomach. He then tied a scarf over her eyes, and she could not see a thing if she wished to.

It was all so . . . exciting.

Next, she felt something warm on her back, the scent of myrrh strong.

"Oil," he said in response to her unasked question.

His large, oiled hands moved over her shoulders, down her spine, over her buttocks, down to just above the stockings, and worked their way back up, sliding between the cheeks of her derrière, to her slit. Victor grinned to himself as she released a moan. He slid a finger in, followed by another, and began pumping inside her. His oiled thumb brushed over her back passage and he felt her stiffen, but only for an instant.

She started to relax, and her soft cry came seconds before her inner muscles clamped around his fingers, her juices coating him.

She strained against the bonds on her arms, and he could see her back rise and fall heavily as she struggled to catch her breath.

Victor climbed onto the bed, his hands moving beneath her spread thighs. Her soft, pink folds were glistening with her dew, and he licked her with intentional softness, the tip of his tongue firm against her clit.

"Oh," she moaned, arching her lower back, giving him better access.

Lillith's hands tightened on the silk binds as liquid fire

rushed through her body, straight to the place Victor stroked her with his velvety tongue.

Her nipples stabbed against the sheets beneath her. She wanted his hands everywhere on her body, needed to feel him inside of her.

Now.

As another climax claimed her, she wanted to tell him no more, that she needed to feel every inch of his cock inside her.

He kissed a path up her spine, his hands moving under her, to her breasts. He cupped her, his fingers playing with her hardened nipples, tugging at them, pinching them with just the right amount of pressure.

She felt his cock against her back, sliding between the cheeks of her ass, grazing her back passage. She held her breath for a moment; then he slid inside her weeping core slowly.

She opened her legs as wide as she could and arched her back to take him as deeply inside as possible.

Victor groaned with satisfaction as he cupped his hips, the head of his cock touching her womb.

Her tight channel gripped him like a hot glove as his balls slapped her folds.

She moved with him, her body craving the friction from the mattress beneath her.

He nuzzled her neck and kissed the curve of her ear, his tongue slipping inside, making the hair on her arms stand on end.

Lillith's insides tightened with each thrust, the touch of his hands on her breasts exquisite, the delicious stroke of his tongue against her neck and ear. She hated the fact she couldn't touch him or even see him, which made her every sense come to life.

He shifted slightly, deliberately positioning himself to where the head of his cock made contact with her sweet spot.

The orgasm was so intense it took her breath away, and she pulled on the bindings as wave upon wave of pleasure washed over her.

A few more thrusts and Victor followed her to paradise, their moans mingling and echoing throughout their new home.

When she finally caught her breath, Victor was untying the binds, starting with the one around her eyes. She blinked a few times, readjusting herself to the light.

"Scandalous man," she said, smiling into his handsome face. He held her close, kissing the top of her head.

"You please me in every way, Lady Graston."

She smoothed her hand over his firm belly, the muscled plane rippling beneath her fingers.

His cock jerked and she looked at him. "Where did you put those binds?" she asked playfully.

"Scandalous woman," he said with a devilish grin.

"I learned from the best," she said with a smile.

Please turn the page
For an exciting sneak peek of
RORY

Coming soon!

1

Rory squinted against the early morning light. Dew glistened on the plush, green lawns, and the first glimmer of sun filtered through the tree branches.

It was a beautiful day to die.

The man at Rory's back started to tremble, and he wondered if the quick-tempered lord wasn't regretting calling him out so hastily. No doubt, like Rory, the earl was replaying last night's events in his head and wishing for a different outcome.

The dinner party had been an elegant affair, and from the moment Rory had walked into Lord and Lady Cordland's townhouse, Lady Cordland had set her sights on him. He had no more taken his seat at the dinner table when her hand had clamped onto his thigh. She had then proceeded to give him a come-hither look that could not be misinterpreted.

When she'd left the table, he followed a discretionary few minutes later, and nearly walked right past her when she reached out and caught him by the arm, jerked him into the parlor, and shoved her hand down his pants.

It had been a fevered and quite exciting coupling, especially given the fact thirty guests chatted and dined on the other side of the wall, including Lady Cordland's husband and his young mistress, his wife's own cousin.

"We can forget about this with an apology," Cordland said in an unsteady voice.

Hell could freeze over before Rory would apologize to the pompous pig. Why was it all right for Cordland to fuck his mistress under his own roof and beneath his wife's nose, but God forbid Lady Cordland do the same?

Rory scanned the park where he had met at least five dozen men in his short life. In the distance he saw a carriage with the Cordland crest emblazoned on the door, and he wondered if Lady Cordland sat within.

Victor, his brother, had recently mentioned Rory's fondness for fucking only married women. A gross exaggeration, but still . . . he did prefer married women because they were *usually* so cautious when compared to their younger counterparts.

"Do I take your silence as acquiescence?" Lord Cordland asked, his voice hopeful.

"My silence means no," Rory replied matter-of-factly, rolling up his sleeves.

Rory's second, an old friend from Cambridge, stood on the sidelines, looking blurry-eyed and terrified that he might have to step in.

He shouldn't be so concerned. Rory had never had to use his second.

"Gentlemen, you will walk off ten paces, and when I say turn, you shall turn and fire," the man in charge said in a booming voice that made Rory cringe. His head still hurt from drinking too much whiskey last night.

Taking a deep breath, Rory released it and lifting the pistol, readied himself for the count.

His hand shook.

Damn, but he was still not thinking clearly. It seemed he had been in a perpetual state of drunkenness since his brothers had married and he had realized how ill his father was.

Life, which had been fun and exciting for so many years, had suddenly turned lonely, mundane, and exceedingly boring, and the future appeared so bleak.

It didn't help his demeanor that his mother was still all over him to wed. Was she really going to force him to marry now that both Sinjin and Victor had done so? In his mind, she was getting greedy. He was the youngest, and had the least to offer a bride, so why did it really matter?

"One, two . . ."

As the count continued, Rory took a step, then another, his mind racing. Life had lost its spark, and he sincerely doubted that finding a wife would help him regain that which he'd lost.

"Eight . . . nine . . . ten!"

The number was shouted and Rory turned, raised his pistol, and for whatever reason—he did *not* pull the trigger.

He heard the roar of his opponent's gun, felt the rip of the bullet tear through his flesh, followed by the sensation of blood seeping through his shirt.

How come he didn't feel any pain?

Lord Cordland's eyes widened when Rory stayed on his feet. Dizziness washed over him, but he fought it off and cocked the hammer.

The man put his hands out and he shook his head. "No, dear God, no!"

There was a second where Rory considered sparing the wretched man's life, and then without thought of consequence, he squeezed the trigger.

Lord Cordland hit the ground with a gasp, the blow fatal, square between the eyes.

"Bloody good shot!" Rory's second yelled as the surgeon

rushed forward, followed by Lord Cordland's second who glared at him.

Glancing down at the blossoming color on his shirt, Rory closed his eyes as a wave of dizziness came over him.

"My lord," the groom said from directly beside him, his voice tinged with concern.

When had he hit the ground? he wondered as the cold, wet grass soaked through his shirt and trousers. He gritted his teeth. Now he was definitely beginning to feel the pain.

"Get the carriage!" he heard the groom yell. Those were the last words he heard before the world went black.

Shannon was concerned when Lord Graston's youngest brother was brought to the manor house on the river Thames with a bullet wound to the shoulder.

Thank goodness the surgeon had done his part by removing the bullet and was at the moment stitching the wound closed. There was not much a person could do now but wait to see if fever took hold. She hoped earnestly that her ministrations would help him, because all of London and Rochester would sincerely feel the young baron's loss if he were to die.

She had experience with injuries since she had volunteered at the local hospital in Dublin. Death had claimed a good number of those patients, and she had seen enough to realize the young man on the bed was gravely ill. His skin had turned a startling gray, and the bullet wound was bright red. He had lost so very much blood that she was concerned he would not survive.

Word had already been sent to Lord Graston in Wales, and the rest of the family would be alerted to Rory's condition, but unfortunately, his brother Sinjin and his wife were on their honeymoon, and his mother, Lady Rochester, was staying close to her ailing husband at their country estate. The poor woman would be sick with grief and worry when she heard the news about her youngest.

Until his family's arrival, the handsome lord would not be lacking in concerned companions. All the female servants in the mansion were already aflutter; each wanting to tend to the handsome lord, but it had been Edward, Lord and Lady Graston's trusted butler who had put Shannon in charge of his care. Upon Rory's arrival in a rented carriage, Edward had lined up the servants and asked who had experience in caring for the wounded. She had immediately raised her hand.

Following Edward into the dining room where Rory had first been brought, Shannon had very nearly tripped over her feet when she'd seen the half-naked lord thrashing on the dining room table, where male servants, including her brother, Zachary, did their best to hold him down.

Rory moaned in his sleep, his handsome face wincing in pain as the doctor applied the bandage. How she wished Lady and Lord Graston were here. She knew his lordship would go to any lengths to save his beloved brother. Until such a time as her employers returned from their trip to Wales, she would have to do her best to keep him alive.

"Make sure the dressing is changed often," the doctor said, putting his items back in his bag. "I shall return tomorrow to check on him."

"Thank you, sir," Edward said, escorting him out of the chamber.

Shannon rinsed the rag in the bowl of cool water that set beside the bed, and looked at her patient. Even pale and wounded, he was beauty personified. A living testament to the male form, so striking he made one pause.

She recalled when last she'd seen him. He'd visited Lady Graston at her London townhouse, and Shannon had served him tea while he awaited Lady Marilyn's arrival. The way he'd watched her through those long, thick lashes had made her nervous. She'd been so dumbstruck by his beauty and attention that it was all she could do to remember her own name. His hair had been long then, but now it was downright rakish, falling past his broad shoulders and curling up at the ends. His nose was perfectly proportioned, his lips full and lovely, and his teeth white and straight.

With a trembling hand, she wiped his brow with the cool rag, past a chiseled cheekbone, over the strong jaw and chin, to his neck. His pulse fluttered erratically at the base of his throat, and she circled it with her index finger.

Her gaze lingered over his wide chest, and flat, muscled belly. She noted a long, silver scar that ran along his ribs, and wondered if, like his current injury, the old wound had been compliments from another woman's husband.

Her cheeks turned pink as her gaze shifted to the sheet that hung low at his hips. Why was it when she was around him she felt hot and sensitive, her nipples tight, and the blood in her veins burned?

She had never been with a naked man before, and as she stared at him, she could not help but wonder what it would feel like to be taken by him, to be one of his many lovers.

Glancing at the sheets bunched about his groin, she once again wet the rag and squeezed out the excess water. Her pulse skittered as her hand moved down the thick cords of his neck, over the wide chest, taking great care to avoid his wound, and swirling around the flat disc of a nipple, before sliding over the muscled planes of his belly.

His cock bucked beneath the sheets. She gasped and swallowed past the tightness of her throat. Before she knew what she was doing, her hand hovered over the sheet, directly above his manhood.

She glanced at the door, and then ever so slightly pulled the sheet down. Her thighs tightened as she stared blatantly at the impressive cock—long and thick, heavily veined with a plum-sized crown. Warmth swirled in her stomach and lower still.

The chamber door creaked open and she jumped, yanking the sheet up with a yelp.

"How is he doing?" Zachary asked, shutting the door firmly behind him.

With heart pumping nearly out of her chest, she released an inward sigh of relief. Thank goodness it was just her brother. Hoping he had not seen what she'd been doing, she licked her dry lips. "It is difficult to say. I just hope he continues to sleep through the night."

"He is fortunate," Zachary said, looking and sounding distracted. "Many would not survive such a wound."

Shannon nodded in agreement and set the rag back into the bowl. "What is it, Zach?"

He pressed his lips together, his chest rising and falling heavily. His throat convulsed as he swallowed hard. "I'm afraid I have grave news, Shannon. I believe Clinton has finally found us."